stones

stones

A NOVEL

WILLIAM BELL

SEAL BOOKS

Seal Books and colophon are trademarks of
Random House of Canada Limited.

STONES
Seal Books/published by arrangement with
Doubleday Canada
Doubleday Canada edition published 2001
Seal Books edition published May 2003

ISBN 0-7704-2875-4

Cover image and design: Daniel Cullen

Seal Books are published by
Random House of Canada Limited.
"Seal Books" and the portrayal of a seal are the property
of Random House of Canada Limited.

Visit Random House of Canada Limited's website:
www.randomhouse.ca

PRINTED AND BOUND IN THE USA

OPM 10 9 8 7 6

part ONE

chapter

It was Ms. Clare who first noticed something was wrong with me. Three times a week she would come into our grade four class and teach us French. She was a short, blonde, overly energetic woman who reminded me of an elf.

After the first day or so, I tuned her out completely. It wasn't anything political; I didn't hate French culture or cooking or the tattered posters of the Louvre and the Eiffel Tower that Ms. Clare had tacked onto the bulletin board beside the display of "Fish of the Great Lakes." It was the repetition and the monotonous chanting. *Bonjour. Comment vous appellez-vous? Je m'appelle Garnet*, and so on. And on and on.

Ms. Clare, in her chirpy new-teacher voice, would lead the recitations, occasionally throwing out a question in French that left us blank-faced and confused, and I would look out the window or draw pictures in my notebook or rest my cheek on my palm and doze. If she spoke to me, I'd ignore her.

One day late in September, Mom and Dad got a letter from the school. Dad tore it open at the kitchen table.

"It says Garnet is hard of hearing," he read. "Or in their words, 'Auditorily differently enabled.' They want to move him to the front of the room and bring in a consultant to test his hearing."

My mother took a sip of her wine. "What's wrong with those people, anyway? Garnet, have you been giving your teacher a hard time?"

I gave her what I hoped was a charming grin and cupped one ear with my hand. "Pardon?" I said.

2

In grade five there was Mr. Whitney, a thin middle-aged man with a face like a horse, who always smelled of cigarettes and cheap after-shave. He would have been happier in the army. He liked to have us line up for this and line up for that, to hand in our notebooks in alphabetical order while he stood at the front of the room tapping a meter stick against the side of his shoe.

In his class, I developed a wander. Right in the middle of a reading session or a science lesson I'd slide out of my chair — a crime equal to murder in Whitney's class — and stand looking out the window or slouch over to the bookshelf where he kept stacks of out-of-date geographic magazines. Whitney would turn pink with rage and order me, "Sit down in your seat and stay there." I always obeyed the first part, but sooner or later I'd be on the move again.

The second letter home of my school career was opened by my mother. She and Dad and I were out on the back porch enjoying a mid-October sunny afternoon.

"It says here that Garnet has ADD," Mom said, squinting at the page in the bright sunlight.

"Which is?" Dad asked, not looking up from the newspaper.

"Which is Attention Deficit Disorder."

"Ah. Which means?"

"Which means, you ignoramus, that he —" here Mom read from the letter, "'can't concentrate or stay on task.'"

"Is this the same boy who can sit in the boat for hours fishing, and not say a word?" Dad asked. "The guy who can while away half a Saturday morning drawing?"

"He's disruptive, according to Mr. Whitney. And disobedient."

Dad cast a critical glance at me. "Well?"

I had been polishing my pocket watch, a present from my parents a couple of years before.

"Disruptive, definitely not. Disobedient, maybe," I said. "What am I supposed to do when he gives us stupid orders?"

"Don't use that word. It's disrespectful."

"Oh, heavens," I said, rolling my eyes dramatically. "A third D."

"And don't be a smart-aleck," Mom put in, not too seriously. "You know what your father means. Mr. Whitney may not be your favorite person —"

"You can say that again."

"— but you have to show respect."

About a week later I was hauled up in front of the principal, who held in his hand a wrinkled piece of paper.

"I take it you drew this," he began.

"Um, possibly."

"It might have been smarter not to sign it," he said sarcastically.

"Does this mean a letter home?"

This one was opened by Dad, and this time we were in the family room. Dad had built a fire, collected the mail and newspaper from the front door, and collapsed onto the sofa, prepared to read for a while. Mom was working on an article for a magazine, tapping away at the computer by the window. Dad read the letter, glanced at the piece of paper that came with it, got up and handed it to Mom.

She started to giggle.

"Now, Annie, how can we discipline this boy if you're not going to be serious?"

The caricature, which I had drawn hastily while Whitney had his back to us writing "Rules for the Field Trip" on the board, showed him sitting on the toilet, boxer shorts around his ankles and a strained look on his face. The caption said, "Maybe you should try working it out with a pencil." It was pretty juvenile, I had to admit.

The cartoon earned me another label: non-compliant.

3

Strangely enough, I graduated, with a diploma signed by the area superintendent and a fairly negative attitude toward my school experience. It hadn't been all bad, but I had never been able, for some reason, to work up the kind of enthusiasm or "school spirit" that a lot of other kids did.

I got one more label before I left Hillcrest Public School.

"It says here he's gifted," Mom read from what I hoped was the final letter home.

Dad yawned. "Really?"

"Yes. They tested him."

"Gifted, eh?"

"Yup."

"Gee, it only took them eight years to find out."

4

High school, which I had naively expected to be exciting, turned out to be anything but. After a terrified year as a niner, which I seemed to spend trying not to get lost in the convoluted halls at

Orillia District Collegiate, and keeping out of the way of older students who treated me with contempt, I sailed across an endless sea of homework questions, tests, projects, and unfocused resentment. I earned a nickname, Lex, in grade ten by asking Ronny Stratton to hand me the lexicon during an English vocabulary exercise.

"What does that mean?" Ronny asked with some irritation.

"Look it up in the lexicon," I said. It had been a joke but Ronny took it as a put-down.

"Oh, yeah. We Earthlings use a dictionary but Garnet uses a *lexicon*."

But the nickname didn't last. You have to be a member of a clique for a nickname to hold. Soon I was Garnet again.

For some reason I had a kind of photographic memory, and I liked to know the origin of words — a strange affliction that I kept to myself. The "gift" my elementary school identified was really a curse. I had learned a long time ago that, if you're really talented at something, most of the teachers seem to want to find a way of showing you you're not as good as you think you are. Not all of them, but most. Mom had told me that was because the teachers felt threatened. The kids would sneer at my high marks, saying I was just sucking up to the teachers.

I could have put up with all that, I guess, if there had been anything going on at school that made it worthwhile, but there wasn't. I stopped being a problem student by grade eleven. From then on, I kept my head down and drifted through the days marking time, waiting to leave.

chapter 2

The high point in my love life occurred when I was in grade one, about five seconds before Evvie McFadden fell into the Christmas tree.

Evvie had a wild swirl of red hair, a button nose sprinkled with freckles and a dimple in the plump flesh above each knee, and I had a crush on her the size of an apartment building. Mrs. Bowles had insisted we all dress up for the Christmas party, so I had on a white shirt and tie, my good pants and real leather shoes with real leather soles. Evvie, in a green dress that beautifully set off her fiery hair, was the prettiest girl in the class.

I watched, my heart aching, as she helped herself to a double-wide piece of chocolate frosted cake and moved near the Christmas tree, where she joined a covey of giggling, whispering girls. Desperate that she notice me for once, I walked over to her, held my breath and, unable to think of anything to say, kicked her in the left shin. The hard edge of my real leather sole went *thunk* as it struck the delicate white skin of her leg.

Evvie's face turned scarlet as her paper plate dropped to the floor and she threw back her head, bawling with gale force, gripping her raised shin with both hands as she hopped in a circle on one foot. The moment I heard that enraged bellow, I fell out of love with her. How could such an ear-splitting howl come from my beautiful, refined Evvie? How could that awkward, thumping, twirling, red-faced creature be thought graceful? The last trace of romance left me when Evvie, still hopping, landed with full force on her own immodestly large piece of cake, slid and collapsed spread-eagle on the Scotch pine, the two of them crashing to the floor in a confusion of glass balls, candy canes, Santa Clauses, angels and tinsel.

After that, my love life went pretty much downhill.

2

It wasn't that I didn't like girls or couldn't get along with them — Rosie Tulipano was one of my best friends until she moved away. It was just that I could never figure out what they wanted. I dated once in a while, but nothing long-lasting came of it. I envied guys who smirked casually in the presence of adoring females, confident in their attractiveness, who moved with easy grace and cracked jokes at will.

There was that one time when I was in grade ten, when I thought I'd died and gone to heaven. Candy Rowe accepted me as her boyfriend. I couldn't understand why she picked me, but I wasn't going to ask any questions. Candy — yeah, that was her name — was curvy and always smelled of make-up and mints. She spoke with breathy exaggeration, flipping her long hair for emphasis.

She hung on me like ivy on brick, insisting that we meet in the hall between classes, where we'd lean on each other, holding hands, nuzzling and kissing, until the bell went — or until a teacher came along and lectured us on "appropriate behaviour." It was after almost a week of this bliss that Candy dumped me. She had been using me to make her former boyfriend jealous. He was one of those jocks whose neck was wider than his head, and student council vice-president. When he came back to her she tossed me into the trash like an empty shampoo bottle.

Talk about a confidence destroyer. I guess my clouded mood was obvious even to my parents.

"What's the matter, dear? You look kind of blue," my mother said.

"Oh, nothing."

"He probably got dumped," Dad quipped.

"As a matter of fact, I did!"

"Gareth, sometimes you can be so insensitive," Mom said.

Dad's face fell. He held his hands out, palms up. "Sorry, Garnet. I was only kidding. I didn't — Um, maybe I'll just go see what's on TV tonight," he said lamely, leaving the room.

Mom shot him a disapproving look as he passed. I stirred my tea some more.

"So, what happened?" Mom asked gently. "Do you want to talk about it?"

"I did get dumped. Again."

"I see."

"I just wish that I was attractive," I said, "like some of the other guys."

Mom took a sip of her tea. She seemed to be thinking something over. Then she said, "You don't know, do you? You really don't."

"Know what?"

"You *are* attractive. No, no, don't give me that look," she said quickly. "I know what you're thinking. 'This is the part where Mom comes along and boosts my flattened ego by telling me I look like a movie star.' But it's the truth. You're not a movie star, but you're a good-looking young man. You're tall, you have a nice face, and you have a cute butt."

"Mom! For —"

"Okay, okay. Sorry. It's the truth, though," she added. The corners of her mouth rose in a devilish smile.

"You're prejudiced. You're my mom — you have to say that. If you're right, I wouldn't be such a loser with girls."

"You want the truth, Garnet? There's more to it than looks. You are attractive, and you're a nice person, but you're kind of shy. You hold back. And girls, well, most of them, the ones your age, are drawn to boys who are, or seem, confident and self-assured. Girls mistake that quality for inner strength. Confidence and strength are sexy."

The conversation was a little embarrassing, but I thought over what she had said for a few minutes. It seemed to fit. Most girls at school went after the jocks, the jokers, the rebels — the ones who seemed to know what they were doing. I had never thought about how I must appear to other people, never looked at myself from someone else's point of view. Who was this guy, Garnet Havelock, and what was he like? I wasn't too happy about the answers that came to mind.

Although I had been a problem student for my first three years, I wasn't a rebel, a guy who got busted for smoking up in the wash-room, for fighting or stealing someone's wallet from the locker room. I wasn't an athlete, that was for sure. And, although school was pretty much a joke to me, I wasn't a joker. Why would anyone be attracted to me? I was like a shadow.

"I guess I'm kind of a nice guy, but a goof, like Dad," I said, meaning nothing negative.

"Don't kid yourself, Garnet. Your dad is one sexy man."

"*Dad?*"

"Yes, your Dad. Haven't you noticed the way women — well, stupid question, of course you haven't. But women find your father very attractive, for all kinds of reasons, believe me. And you have a lot of his qualities."

I laughed. "Including a cute butt?"

"Now you're getting it. Listen, Garnet. Try not to be discouraged. Don't chase after empty-headed females who get all twittery when a football player walks by. You'll do okay. Just try to be patient."

3

After Candy, I guess I became cynical, in spite of Mom's attempt to buck me up. I didn't trust girls, or my own feelings for that matter. And the more I thought about it, the less I believed in love. At least, that was what I told myself. The relationships on TV and in the movies always seemed brief and intense and entirely physical, a kind of mutual exploitation. The people "loved" each other — for a while, any-way — but they didn't seem to *like* each other. Their idea of commitment was "as long as it works for me." And at school it was "as long as you make me look good."

The whole thing was too confusing.

So I wasn't exactly thrilled when Mr. Paulsen, our English teacher, announced the weekly Great Debate topic. Resolved: that love at first sight is a hoax.

"What does hoax mean?" someone shouted.

Paulsen was a nice guy but not too good at controlling a class.

"Ask Garnet," someone else said, getting a laugh.

"A con, a scam, a deception," I said.

Ordinarily I didn't care what the resolution of the debate was. I barely paid attention during those times, preferring to doodle in my notebook or draw furniture designs or read a novel. But this time I was to be one of the speakers. It was my turn. And I needed the marks.

"Garnet, you and Randy are pro," Paulsen shouted over the noise.

Well, it could have been worse. I had to prove that love at first sight was phoney. I could have ended up con, trying to argue that love at first sight was real, and I was probably the last person in the universe to believe that.

4

Love at first sight — what a crock. The whole notion had probably been dreamed up by some tenth-rate dramatist back in the old days, some loser with a quill pen who needed to move the story along quickly and was too lazy or unimaginative to develop a believable love affair between his characters. So he wrote a scene where the man and woman catch sight of each other across a busy street or a crowded drawing room and BANG, they're in love. Sure.

There were all kinds of things wrong with the scenario. First, how could you love someone you didn't know? You'd be completely ignorant of their personality. Maybe you just fell head over heels for a total bore, a real snooze-monger whose idea of excitement was reading the fine print on an insurance policy. Or maybe you were dazzled by a serial killer — how would you have known? — with the smell of his latest kill in his nostrils and blood on his hands. Or you were all hot to give your heart to this stranger but nobody told you she liked the same gender you did.

Second, love at first sight had to be strictly physical, but everybody said that love was more than that. How could it be, if you fell in love without speaking a word? I didn't buy it. Love at first sight was all fairy-land and movies and bad novels with pictures on the cover of nurses gazing into the eyes of firm-jawed doctors.

I believed in logic, reason, science, hard fact — which was why I disliked poetry. I read a lot, non-fiction and fiction (but never romances). I wanted a good story, or information, not dreams and gooey sentiment about moonlight and fields of flowers and Gee, isn't that a lovely sunset.

For the debate, the difficulty was to get my thoughts in order so I wouldn't make a fool of myself — I hated talking in front of others — and maybe I could salvage my English mark.

chapter **3**

"But what about Romeo and Juliet?"

"What about them?"

"Well, it should be obvious, even to you. They fell in love at first sight. At the Capulet party. And later they were married by Friar What's-his-name. So, if they experienced love at first sight, it must be real. They're famous."

André, a skinny straw-haired guy, sat down, bathed in background noise, looking pleased with himself. Randy jumped to his feet again.

"Not so fast. Juliet was fourteen, and Romeo wasn't much older. You can't build your argument on the actions and feelings of two bone-headed teenagers who ended up dead through their own stupidity. Besides, they weren't real. They're characters in a *play*. We're debating real life here."

Randy dropped into his seat, accepting high-fives from the guys around him, preening like the only rooster in the barnyard and playing with the rings in his ear. The two sides flung insults at each other. A paper ball sailed across the room and was batted back to its owner. In the clamour, the classroom door opened and someone slipped in. I paid no attention. I was psyching myself up.

"Garnet, your turn," Paulsen shouted. "The rest of you, pipe down!"

I got ready to slay them with logic, knock down their arguments like bowling pins. No sticky romantic mumblings or passions of the heart. Clear thinking. In my room the night before, it had sounded good.

"Mr. Speaker," I began with a squeak. Someone laughed. I cleared my throat. "Mr. Speaker, this is simply a matter of sound logic, a quality which my opponents have never heard of."

Hissing and catcalls from the opposition. Cheers from my side. Paulsen liked it when we sounded arrogant.

"All of us here today, even my opponents, with their diminished mental capacity, would agree that true love is both physical *and* spiritual. Now, love at first sight is, by definition, love

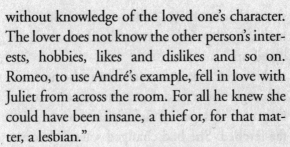

without knowledge of the loved one's character. The lover does not know the other person's interests, hobbies, likes and dislikes and so on. Romeo, to use André's example, fell in love with Juliet from across the room. For all he knew she could have been insane, a thief or, for that matter, a lesbian."

An uproar. Groans and giggles from both sides. Paulsen shot me a harsh look, then tried to quiet the class down.

"Since he had never so much as spoken to her," I went on, "his so-called love for her must have been based on physical appearance alone. Obviously, the same goes for her."

I paused for dramatic effect. "And, since true love is, as I have said, physical *and* spiritual, Romeo and Juliet could not have been experiencing true love. What they felt was lust. They wanted to get inside each other's clothes. Period. The spiritual element was missing."

The hubbub swelled once more. "Love at first sight," I strained to make myself heard above the roar, "is a hoax!"

They think I'm debating, I thought, but I meant every word I said.

The din continued. A couple of paper airplanes took off and crash-landed. Paulsen

shouted something. At the front of the classroom, by the desk next to the door, someone
stood up.

None of us knew much about the new kid,
although there had been the usual swirl of
rumours — some of them pretty nasty, some
far-fetched. She had changed schools because
of conflicts with other students. She'd been
expelled for poor attendance. Jill, who considered a tasty morsel of gossip sweeter than a
candy bar, had told us Raphaella's mother
owned the health food store and that the
word was, Raphaella never dated. "She's
weird," Jill had concluded. "I mean, what
kind of name is that? And they tell me she
belongs to some cult or other." Raphaella had
transferred to our school from Park Street
Collegiate about a week before — just in time
to be assigned a role in the debate — then
had disappeared.

When she got to her feet, something
remarkable happened. She stood quietly, completely at ease, and waited. Normally, a new kid
gives off vibes like a high-tension wire — fear,
embarrassment, a pathetic desire to be accepted. Not this one. Wearing a long navy blue
dress over a black T-shirt, a silver-colored ankh

hanging from a leather thong around her neck, she appeared calm — except for her bitten-down fingernails — and completely indifferent to us. She was slender, a bit taller than me, with glossy black hair that fell almost to her waist. A plum-colored birthmark stained her neck and half her right cheek.

I felt something shift inside me, a kind of low-level seismic tremor.

Gradually, as she waited patiently, the noise around her ebbed away. It was as if she had taken control of the room without effort. Everyone, including Paulsen, stared at her. Nobody moved.

She lifted a piece of paper from her desk, consulted it and put it down. She never referred to it again.

She turned her gaze on me. Unblinking. Straight into my eyes.

"Logic is only one way of looking at the world," she said, "and it's very limited. It's like looking at life through binoculars held the wrong way around."

A murmur ended almost as soon as it began.

"Your argument sounds *reasonable*" — she said the word as if it were a minor obscenity — "but only if we accept the idea that there is only one kind of knowledge, the kind based on direct experience. Juliet and Romeo had never met before her father's masquerade. Therefore, according to you, they could not know each other. Therefore, what they felt was only physical desire, not love."

She paused. Some of the students around her traded smirks that revealed their inability to follow her argument.

"Unfortunately," she continued in the same confident tone, "your idea is wrong. There is more than one kind of knowledge. Or, as Hamlet put it, 'There are more things in heaven and earth, Horatio, than are dreamt of in your philosophy.'"

"Like what?" Randy sneered. "Horoscopes and oracles?"

"I mean intuition, spontaneous insight. Romeo and Juliet *knew* each other in a split second of revelation. When they had a chance to talk —"

"Yeah, all that 'Pilgrim' stuff," André cut in.

"— they were able to confirm what they already knew, that the other person was worthy of being loved. The balcony scene allowed them to explore each other even more."

There were a few snickers at the word "explore."

"Intuition and revelation aren't knowledge," I insisted. "They're for religion and mysticism. They're just . . . well . . . feelings."

"You guys always say that," Janet Bilisis remarked from the corner of the room, always the feminist. Her nose stud twinkled. "You can't accept —"

"Oh, here we go again." This from Randy. "It's a girl thing, is it? Only girls get it? Garnet is right. Admit it."

"If it *is* a girl thing," Janet seethed, "that's only because you guys are such emotional cripples that you can't feel *anything*."

Confusion. Insults and lame jokes darted back and forth.

Raphaella waited once more until quiet returned. "If they *are* just feelings, as you put it, they're still knowledge. There is such a thing as emotional knowledge. Face it," she said, once again training those large, dark, soft eyes on me. "Love at first sight is valid. It's real. People fall in love every day. Science can't explain it, except to make numb comments about biological urges. Science can't explain most things that are important."

She sat down gracefully, ignoring the groundswell of talk that surged around her. Even before she finished talking, I had fallen in love with her.

All weekend, I couldn't get her out of my mind. This is crazy, I kept telling myself. This is stupid. I must have food poisoning. Can you get hardening of the arteries in the brain before you finish high school?

In my workshop at the rear of my family's antique store I fussed and puttered aimlessly among cans of wood stain, varnish and solvent, afraid to work on a difficult restoration in case I split the wood or cut my thumb off. I went for walks, hoping each time I turned a corner I'd run into her. I strolled casually past the Demeter health food store, stealing glances through the window, searching for her willowy form, her long dark hair.

Monday morning I actually made it to school on time. I stalked the halls between classes and at lunch period, trying to fake a chance meeting, mentally rehearsing what I would say. The day dragged until final class — English. I entered the room with forced nonchalance, my stomach in a knot, my nerves jangling like a ring of old keys. She didn't show.

She came to English on Tuesday to write a test and didn't so much as glance my way. She finished early and disappeared. I flunked the test.

The torture went on all week. I didn't dare ask anyone for her last name because I couldn't face the ridicule — "She creamed you in the debate and now you want to romance her, Garnet?", "I guess love at first sight works for *some* people!" — so looking her up in the phone book was impossible, even if I could get up the nerve to call.

Finally, after the final class on Friday had inched to an end without her turning up, I walked down West Street and along Mississauga to our store, closed myself in the office and picked up the phone.

"Hello. Park Street Collegiate. How may I help you?"

In my most businesslike voice: "Guidance office secretary, please."

"One moment."

"Guidance office. Mrs. Connor speaking."

"Good afternoon. It's Stanley Paulsen over at O. D. I have a new student who has just transferred and her student record hasn't arrived yet."

"Yes?"

"I just want to check that she has the prerequisite to take this course. Her name is . . . let me see, where did I put the paperwork?" I rustled a few invoices Dad had piled on the desk. "The name is unusual. Um, Raphaella? Oh, where's that damn class list gone?"

"Skye. Raphaella Skye."

"Ah, yes. Of course. And it's spelled?"

"With an *e*."

"Right. Oh, for heaven's sake! I have the record right here. Sorry to trouble you."

I hung up. A quick look at the phone book. One listing for Skye, in Orillia.

I got up from the desk and stalked back and forth for a few minutes, psyching myself as I had for the debate. I went back to the phone and keyed in the number. I hoped my voice hadn't become a mousey squeak.

"Hello?" I heard. It wasn't her.

"Hi, could I speak to Raphaella, please."

"Who's calling?" she demanded with the warmth of a morgue attendant.

"A friend from school. Garnet."

A rustle and a scratchy sound told me the woman was holding her hand over the receiver. "It's some guy named Gannet."

"No, no!" I said. "It's *Gar*net."

"Never heard of him." Raphaella's voice, muffled by the woman's hand on the mouthpiece.

"Says he's a friend from school."

"I don't know any Gannet. A gannet's a *bird*."

"Garnet!" I shouted. "It's Garnet. G-A-R —"

"Are you going talk to him or not?"

"No, thanks. I've had enough crap from those jerks at Park. And I don't know anyone at O. D. Especially a seabird. Tell whoever it is to migrate."

"She's not here," the voice told me.

"My name's *Garnet*," I repeated. "We're in the same English class. We were in the debate together."

The woman gave out an exasperated "Tsk!" and reluctantly conveyed the information. By then I had completely lost my courage. My throat went dry. I was about to write the whole thing off and hang up when I heard, "Hello?" It was Raphaella.

"Er, hi. It's Garnet Havelock. I'm in Paulsen's English class. And I'm not a seagull."

Silence. So much for my killing sense of humor.

"The debate?" I prompted. "We were on opposite sides?"

"Oh, I remember."

"Well, um, I just called to see if, well, you'd be interested in maybe, you know, having a cup of coffee or something, sometime."

"I don't drink coffee."

This is like mining coal, I thought. "Well, it doesn't have to be *coffee*. I mean, tea, a soft drink, anything."

"I don't think so. But thanks anyway, Gannet."

"Okay, well, goodbye, then."

"Bye."

I slammed down the phone in frustration, Garnet Havelock, Mr. Cool. Mr. Romance. Mr. Total Loser.

2

How my parents ever managed to get together and stay that way was beyond me.

If you had looked up "introverted" in the

dictionary you'd have found my father's picture, a shy, half-apologetic smile on his face. Unassuming and friendly. A receding hairline, a bit overweight. He had his feet stuck firmly in the mud. For him, the hour-and-a-half drive to Toronto was a major safari.

My mother, a slender, fair-haired bundle of nervous energy, was born with itchy feet. She was a freelance journalist, most alive when she was in the thick of international conflict, national disaster, political scandal. She was famous for her pitiless analysis and piercing questions, a kind of butterfly with a sting. Sometimes, she was away for weeks on end. She'd come back frazzled and worn down, exhilarated and exhausted, drop her bags in the front hall and announce, "Boy, am I glad to be home!" and crash. But sooner or later her eyes would take on that faraway look, she'd go for long walks, and eventually she'd pick up the phone, call her contacts at newspapers and magazines, scratching for an assignment, and take wing like a migrant bird.

Dad's unspoken motto was, Old Is Good, New Is No Good. He liked old cars, old tunes, old books, old movies. Words and phrases like "groovy" or "snazzy" flavored his speech, and he liked to imitate characters from classic cinema. The only trouble was, nobody knew who he was impersonating, so the effect was lost. He didn't care.

Dad taught music at a couple of elementary schools in the mornings. He enjoyed working with the rug-rats and ankle-biters, but his real love was Olde Gold Antiques and Collectibles, the shop we owned on Mississauga Street across from the library and the opera house. It was open on weekdays from one o'clock, and all day Saturday, when I ran the store myself. Dad liked to scan the newspaper Friday night and make a list of garage sales running the next day. He'd tear around town from place to place in his refurbished 1966 Chevy pickup looking for bargains.

"You'd be surprised what kind of stuff people sell at those sales," he would say to Mom every once in a while.

"I don't think I would be," Mom would reply sarcastically. Then she'd repeat her theory that people who went to garage sales searching for bargains eventually collected so much junk they had to hold one themselves. Then others came along and bought back their own stuff and the cycle would start over.

Old things, recycled ideas, drove her nuts. Being a journalist, she was always frantic to know what was new, the latest scoop, the breaking story — and sometimes she brought these things to light herself. Her reports were widely admired, and Dad and I sometimes heard her interviewed — always in five- or ten-second sound bites — on the radio or TV. Once we saw her on the tube, standing in the center of an African refugee camp that the opposing army had threatened to attack, surrounded by rake-thin victims of civil war whose hollow eyes showed their desperation. Dad kept all Mom's written reports in a big scrapbook, despite her reminders that everything she wrote was on disk.

"I don't trust electronics," he would say.

I was never certain whether I had inherited the best from each of them or the worst. For as long as I could remember I'd had a raging curiosity about things, an endless thirst for answers (this from my mother) — which made fitting in at school pretty hard most of the time.

At the antique store, I was the official Olde Gold restorer and refinisher. In the back was a workshop with a lathe, a workbench, saws, planes, chisels and what-all. If a piece of furniture came in with a splintered rail or leg, a smashed or missing drawer, I made new ones. For me, raising the grain in a piece of oak or pine with sandpaper, stain and plastic finish, or turning a chair rail in bird's-eye maple or cherry wood brought greater satisfaction than an A on a test. This from my father.

When I was in grade nine, I asked out a girl named Sandy Mills. She had been named athlete of the year at Hillcrest Public School the year before and had a high opinion of herself. I had a high opinion of her too; she was pretty, smart and popular. When I invited her to go to the movies she said she couldn't let me know until Friday. Having no choice, I said okay. I was grateful for the possibility. We went out and we both had a good time. The following Monday, I asked her again. Same response. On Friday night she agreed to have dinner at the Bay Burger, then go to the movies again. I finally found out why she would put me off until Friday before committing herself. She was waiting to see if Tony Randall, who was in grade eleven, would ask her out. If nothing developed by Friday she would say yes to me.

I was her backup boyfriend. Try that for a morale killer.

When I was little, I had felt that way about Dad and me. We were Mom's backup life. If nothing was happening with her job, she'd be with us, but it always seemed that her career had priority. As I grew older I got over that feeling and I understood Mom more. She was ambitious, not just for herself but for me as well.

So she wasn't happy when, one day early in my final year of high school, I let her in on *my* ambition. I waited until she was in the middle of a feature article she was writing for a national magazine. Something about election corruption in provincial politics. I figured if she was a little distracted I might be able to sneak the notion past her.

"Um, Mom, this might not be the best time to talk about it, but I want to try out an idea on you."

"Oh," she said, typing away, "what?"

"First you have to promise me you won't get mad."

She stopped tapping and turned to me. "Garnet, don't be so dramatic. Let's hear it." When I said nothing, she relented. "All right. I won't get angry."

"I've decided I don't want to go on after high school."

She clicked on the Save button and stared at the screen.

"Don't you want to hear my reasons?"

"No, I don't, Garnet. You want to throw away your future, become a dropout."

"Mom, I hate school so much. As it is, every morning I have to drag myself up the hill, sit through incredibly boring classes that have nothing to do with anything. It's not like I don't know what I want to do with my life. I do. And I don't need a degree for it. I want to get on with things."

"Your father and I always hoped you'd go to university."

"No, you did."

"Whatever. And now you'll be a quitter."

"I'm not quitting. You're twisting things. I told you a million times, I know what I want to do in life. I'm not quitting. I want to *begin*."

"Well, it's not a good idea and I'm not going to support it."

"Mom, how come it's all right for Dad and me to support your career, but when it's my turn, it's a different story?"

My plan was to finish high school and work at the store full time while I found a cabinet-maker to apprentice myself to, then one day open my own shop where I could design and build furniture. Dad loved the idea; Mom didn't. She wanted me to go to university first, to "keep my options open."

They couldn't even agree on my future. But there was one thing about the two of them. They loved each other so deeply you'd have sworn they were wired to the center of the universe.

chapter

The six-o'clock news was just coming on when I left Toronto and joined the rush-hour traffic heading north on Highway 400. I had spent the entire day, almost, delivering a pine dresser — refinished by You Know Who — to a customer who lived, in Dad's vague directions, "somewhere off the Danforth." It had taken me an hour just to find the house.

It was a cold day in late March, blustery and damp. The sky was the color of wet cement, and flakes of snow, riding sluggishly on a damp wind, flecked the windshield and melted immediately. When the news was over, the weather woman sent out dire warnings about a freak storm, as if a snowfall came only once each century.

As I made my way north, snow began to coat the shoulders of the road, then gradually crept toward the center in spite of the volume of traffic. As the snow built up, the traffic slowed, and four lanes caved in to three, then two, then one long slow-moving line.

By the time I came to the strip malls and factories a few miles south of Barrie it was dark and I was in the middle of a full blizzard, peering through a white fog of snow at the tail lights of the cars in front of me. The wind howled across the highway, pushing curtains of thick flakes, picking up snow from the fields and banks on the west side of the road and stirring it into the storm, producing a white-out. Driving in the white-out was like creeping along the bottom of a sea of milky water that was constantly swirling and buffeting the van, reducing visibility to zero.

I was sneaking along at about twenty klicks an hour, leaning forward, my hands clenched on the steering wheel. Suddenly red lights appeared ahead of me, flashing on and off in a broad band. I flipped on my emergency flashers and gingerly applied the brakes, my shoulders hunched in anticipation of another car smashing into the back of me. I came to a halt without sliding.

I strained to see ahead. There appeared to be a clear track along the divider. I moved forward slowly, threading a needle. In a Ford Bronco that was facing backwards, a man was talking into a cell phone. A bunch of kids in a van sat with faces glued to the glass. Six or seven cars, pointing in every direction, lay slammed together like toys left behind in the middle of a living room. I passed an ambulance. One of the paramedics was walking from car to car; the other was talking on the radio. A tractor-trailer had jackknifed and swept half a dozen cars into the ditch.

Soon I cleared the wreckage. The highway ahead seemed almost empty after the mess I had come through.

I continued, took Highway 11, climbed the rise to "gasoline alley," where the gas station lamps were amber blobs in the fog of snow, then fishtailed my way up the long hill north of the alley. Completely unnerved by then, I decided to get off the highway at the Third Concession, if I could find it.

I knew that the concession road hooked up with the Old Barrie Road, which I could follow into Orillia. There were farms all along the route, so I wouldn't be trapped or isolated if the roads proved to be impassable.

I pushed on. The radio said that almost a meter of snow had fallen in the last three hours. The heater fan roared, the wipers flapped frantically, barely able to keep ahead of the snow, my hands ached from gripping the wheel, my neck and shoulders were stiff from tension.

The van began to slither around like an eel as it pushed through the deepening snow, steadily losing traction. Without warning, it shied sideways when the rear wheels broke free. I eased off the gas, almost out of control, as the van tried to swap ends. It lurched to the right, and the steering wheel whipped from my hands. The van dipped forward, then a huge black shape loomed ahead, seeming to rise up out of the whirling blanket of white. I hit the brakes too late and heard a dull metallic crunch. My body pitched forward and I felt my breath whoosh out as the seat belt yanked against my chest.

The engine stalled. I forced myself to take a deep breath. The left headlight had smashed in the collision with what looked like a stone wall that rose to the height of the windshield. The right headlight tore a tunnel through the thicket of snow, revealing nothing.

When I had my breathing under control I started the van and tried to back out onto the road. The rear wheels spun uselessly. I tried rocking the van back and forward, switching rapidly from Reverse to Drive. I got nowhere. Cursing, I shut off the engine. Over the tick of the cooling motor the howling wind told me I had a serious challenge on my hands, stranded until daylight or until the snow stopped and a plow came by. In my mind I ran a check on the items in what Dad called the disaster kit we keep behind the seat: an anorak, boots, hat, mitts, a cold-weather sleeping bag, matches, a flashlight. I opened the glove compartment and took out the cell phone. With a cheerful beep and a blinking black triangle in the display window, it told me the battery was dead.

I was in deep trouble. Sitting in the van for hours with the engine running was not an option, unless I wanted to gas myself to death. Neither was flirting with hypothermia. I turned off the headlights and the night closed in around me.

I reached behind the seat, unzipped the canvas bag and lifted out the flashlight, a long tubular model like the ones cops use. Shining it through the windshield was impossible. The glass threw the light back, making my eyes smart in the glare. I rolled down the door window, stuck my arm into the freezing wind, playing the flashlight beam back and forth. Snow swirled into the cab. The light revealed a structure made of large stones and mortar.

The icy wind quickly coated the inside of the windshield with condensation, which immediately froze. I stuck my head out the window, swept back and forth with the light again. Let there be a house or something nearby, I whispered. The gusts rose and fell, buffeting the van, stinging my face with snow, numbing my hands.

Then I saw something. Something that flashed whiter than the snow, a broken outline of an octagon. A stop sign.

I pulled my arm, now caked with snow, inside and rolled up the window. By now I could see my breath. I pulled the disaster kit from behind the seat, telling myself I'd be all right, turning my options over in my mind as I pulled on a wool toque, a goose-down vest and waterproof anorak, and heavy felt-lined boots. I stuffed the wool-lined leather mitts into the pockets of the anorak.

A stop sign indicated a crossroads. Four corners often meant buildings, but there were no lights, not even a glimmer in the wall of flying snow. Probably the hydro was out — a good possibility, given the power of the wind. But even if the electricity was off, there would be candlelight, lanterns, something. Maybe, I thought as my spirits fell again, it was only a crossroads. Should I risk getting lost stumbling around in the gale, searching for a shed or a barn, or should I stay in the van and try to keep myself from dying from the cold?

Always stay with the boat was a rule drummed into my head every summer when I went to camp on the other side of Lake Couchiching. If your canoe overturns, if your sailboat capsizes, never try to swim for shore. Stay with the boat. Always. No exceptions. You'll be tempted to swim for it. Don't.

So I'd stay with the van. But I could try to probe the snowfall with the flashlight, get a better look. I turned on the parking lights to give me a point of orientation once I was outside, pulled up my hood, tied the strings under my chin and put on the heavy mitts. I slid over to the passenger side, pushed open the door and got out, sinking to my knees. With a gnawing sense of futility, I shone the flashlight into the storm. I saw nothing but a shifting white wall, then the luminescent outline of the stop sign winked in and out of view with the pulsing of the wind. I scoured to the right of the sign. Gradually, though the surging and waning of the blizzard, something seemed to form itself. It was a small building.

Leaning into the wind, I waded back to the lee side of the van. From under the seat I took a length of rope I had used to tie down the dresser. I secured one end to the door handle, grabbed the survival kit, which now contained only the sleeping bag, and, playing out the rope as I went, stumbling through drifts toward the building.

I found the door easily enough, kicked snow out of the way, pulled it open to reveal an inner door. It was locked.

I tied the rope to the skeleton of a bush and stashed the bag between the doors to keep it dry. Then, guided by the rope, I plowed back to the van. I turned off the parking lights. The wind had picked up, and by the time I had returned to the door with a tire iron my teeth were chattering. If I was lucky, the cabin would have a fireplace or stove.

A few blows with the tire iron tore the rusted hasp out of the door frame and the lock dropped to my feet. I stepped inside and pulled the doors shut. I was safe.

The cabin — or whatever it was — had one room, about ten feet by twelve, with a dozen or so benches in the middle, most of them arranged in two banks with an aisle up the middle, a few overturned. Some kind of meeting house, I figured. The still, frigid air, the inky black at the edge of the pool of light cast by the flashlight, the shadows that stretched away from me across the floor and up the walls combined to create an eerie atmosphere.

I stood by the door and played the light around the room. The side walls had two large windows each, made up of square panes. At the far end of the room was a table, and in the corner lay a broken lectern. The wall showed the faint outline of a large cross.

Now I knew what kind of meeting place it was.

I said a silent Hooray when I caught sight of a small stove and a stack of wood in the corner. My footsteps thumped hollowly on the wooden floor, my breath formed frost clouds before me. As I neared one of the windows I took a look outside.

A hooded figure stood out there, watching me.

The flashlight crashed to the floor and rolled away, the light beam wobbling crazily until it came to rest, sending a streak of light up the wall where the cross had hung. I stood frozen to the spot, heart hammering.

The window was dark again and I saw nothing. I side-stepped slowly over to the flashlight. I stayed clear of the beam so whoever was out there couldn't see me. When my brain began to function again I realized that whoever it was would need to come in.

But who was he? What was he doing, on foot, out in the storm? I bent slowly and picked up the flashlight. "Who's there?" I called out. Then, louder, "Is there someone out there?"

No answer, only the sighing wind. I crept slowly to the window and, summoning my courage, raised the light to the glass. He was still there, motionless. Terrified again, I forced myself to examine him. He wore an anorak with the hood laced under his chin.

"You idiot," I said out loud.

The flashlight had turned the window into a mirror. I was looking at my own reflection.

Muttering angrily at myself, feeling foolish but unable to shake the sense of uneasiness, I dragged two benches to the corner and spread out the sleeping bag, shaking it to give it loft. Then I opened the stove door and shone the light inside. It seemed functional. Beside it was a wooden box containing kindling and newspaper, and beside that a small stack of split wood. If I was economical, it would last the night. I set paper and kindling in the stove and heard the roar of flame and smoke sucked up the chimney and away by the wind.

I kicked off my boots, shrugged out of the anorak and climbed into the sleeping bag. Soon the warmth began to make me sleepy. The next day the snowplows would be out. I'd walk the road until I came to a house, call for a tow truck to pull the van out of the ditch, drive home, get some hot coffee into me, have a long, hot shower.

The wind howled along the walls of the old church, moaned at the eaves, whined at the window ledges, fistfuls of snow rattling the glass. As it warmed, the building creaked and cracked.

My thoughts turned to Raphaella. I pictured her standing in class during the debate, her pale skin and dark eyes, the plum-colored mark on her face and neck. I saw her walking down the hall, her long black hair swaying to and fro across her back. Her willowy body. She carried herself with a confidence and grace I hardly ever saw in other girls. She was intelligent and articulate and wasn't afraid to show it.

No wonder I was in love with her. I ached to see her again, close-up this time. But how could I manage it?

I got up and put another small log on the fire. I scrunched down into the sleeping bag and, with her face in my imagination, fell asleep.

2

Once, a few years before, I had a vicious case of bronchitis that brought with it a high fever and bizarre, terrifying nightmares that left me breathless and sweaty. In the church, with the blizzard raging outside and hard benches under me, I slept fitfully, slipping in and out of troubling dreams. Though I couldn't recall it, each dream left a residue of dread that seemed to build as the night wore slowly on, until finally I was awakened by the rasping of my own rapid breathing.

Around me the rushing wind shrieked and moaned. The comforting crackle of the fire had died away. I swallowed on a dry throat, fumbled for the flashlight and checked my watch. It was just after two o'clock.

Gradually, like a theme emerging in a piece of music, a sound borne by the wind began to separate itself from the background howl. I strained to identify it, scarcely breathing, rigid with concentration. An insistent grumble, like a crowd makes in a movie or a play.

The grumbling intensified without being louder, became more human, the voices of men, at least half a dozen, double that at most. Their distant murmuring carried tones of anger, determination, fear. The sound swelled, stronger, more insistent. Then, like bubbles rising to the surface, one at a time, and bursting, I heard *eighty wish . . . now . . . go back! . . . no!*, each distinct word floating on a rumbling tide of rage and terror and, finally, hatred.

Eighty wish . . . go back! . . . no! Then, *Stone
. . . stone.*

It was as if the men were passing outside the church on their way somewhere.

The voices receded into the roar of the storm. I was half free of the sleeping bag, propped on one elbow, straining after the terrible sounds. I lay down again, trembling. I began to reason with myself, word by unspoken word regaining confidence. I was imagining things. A gusty wind like that could make strange effects, play with my mind. There were no men. How could there be, in a storm like this in the middle of the night? My nightmares, the stress of the day, loneliness and isolation had gotten to me. Hadn't I thought I saw a man in the window a few hours before?

I took in a long breath and let it out slowly. Be reasonable, I repeated to myself. I wanted to go back to sleep, but in a way I was afraid to. There's nothing to fear, I told myself. Don't be a fool.

3

Three times that night the voices returned. By the time a weak grey light diluted the darkness at the windows the wind had ceased its assault on the cabin, and I was a wreck.

When the light had risen enough to illuminate the inside of the church, I got up, made sure the fire in the stove was out, packed up my stuff and pushed open the door. The driven snow had been sculpted into ridges like frozen waves alongside and behind the building. In the flat light of early morning I saw that the log structure stood at the intersection of the Third Concession and the Old Barrie Road. Nearby was a stone monument, and on its far side rested the van, its left front smashed in.

Unable to stop myself, I searched the drifts around the church for footprints. I found nothing. Coiling my guide rope, I plowed my way to the van and stowed my gear behind the seat.

The engine started immediately and, with the heater pumping warm air into the cab, I tried once more to back out onto the road. No luck.

An hour or so later a county snowplow came by, snorting diesel smoke into the cold, still air, the blue light revolving on the top. The driver was happy to pull me out of the ditch. I followed the plow into town, glad to see the red streak of the rising sun in the trees beside the road.

chapter 7

By failing to come home the night of the blizzard I had thrown a scare into my parents, and, as usual, they eased their nerves by ranting — after hugging and fussing over me when I walked into the house that morning. Then they ganged up on me as I was sipping a welcome cup of hot tea at the kitchen table.

"Why didn't you call?" Mom demanded.

"That's what the phone is for," Dad put in.

"Yeah, but the battery was flat."

"So? You could have recharged it from the cigarette lighter."

"I forgot the adapter."

Mom was leaning on the counter, arms crossed. "You drove off to the city without the adapter. Into the biggest storm in ten years. *With* the cell phone, *without* the adapter."

"Don't rub it in. I didn't know it was going to snow."

Dad added, "I keep telling you, don't drive any distance in the winter without checking the Weather Channel first."

I stood up. "I'd love to stay and let you two hammer away at me some more, but I'm going to have a long, hot shower instead."

"Take the phone with you," Dad said, and all three of us burst out laughing.

2

Olde Gold Antiques and Collectibles was a narrow, two-storey red-brick building with The Magus, a bookstore, on one side and an espresso bar on the other. The store occupied the main floor, with a showroom at the front, a small office and a workshop out back. Overhead was a stamped-tin ceiling, thick with many coats of paint, and the floor was made of pegged oak planks. There was a cellar, dark and creepy, where the bathroom was and where we stored pieces waiting to be refinished or repaired.

Business was transacted in a time warp: cash only, unless the customer was local; then we would take a check. Each sale was recorded on an invoice, white copy for the buyer, yellow for us, and rung up on a huge ancient cash register with heavy nickel-plated trim. When the big round keys were pressed, labels popped up into a window, showing the amount of the sale, and the contraption let out a *ring!* that they could probably hear across the street in the library. There was no computer, no credit cards, Air Miles, special offers, coupons or mailing lists, no money-back guarantee.

"Buy it, give us the money, and keep it" was Dad's retailing motto.

I worked there on Saturdays, opening up at ten and closing at five. I usually had the place to myself. When she wasn't off chasing a story, Mom would be at home and Dad was usually on the road hunting up treasures at auctions and garage sales. There was a brass bell hanging over the front door that summoned me from the workshop when somebody came in.

I liked the job. There had been a time when I'd had a burst of independence, insisting on a "real job" somewhere outside the family business. I found one, at a department store in the mall. After I'd been there a couple of months the manager told me to follow an old woman around the store and keep an eye on her. She was wearing a ratty old cloth raincoat with a scarf on her head. A toddler, wearing clothes that were too small for him, stood in the shopping cart, pretending to pilot it through the store as his grandmother pushed. I watched the woman pocket a kid-size toothbrush, a comb with a cartoon character head on it, a packet of gum. She got on the elevator and I slipped in just as the door was closing.

"They're watching you," I said to the doors. "They know what you're doing."

She rode the elevator back down, got off and put all the stuff back. It touched me when she did that. She could have dumped the items on the elevator floor or laid them on a shelf somewhere and walked away. They caught her putting the comb back in the display case. Security had called the cops.

When the manager ordered me to tell Security what I had seen I said, "Nothing." Red-faced and cursing, he fired me on the spot. When I left the store, the old lady and her grandson were sitting in the back of a police car. I guessed I wasn't hard-hearted enough for the commercial world.

Anyway, on a sunny Saturday a week or so after the blizzard, I opened the store as usual.

Cars hissed past, throwing dirty slush to the edge of the sidewalk, and shoppers walked briskly in the chilly air. Across the street the giant icicles hanging from the eaves of the opera house were turned to crystal by the morning sun.

I put a Mozart CD on the stereo and switched on the electric heater in the shop. Then I ducked into the espresso bar for a double-shot latte, took it back to the shop and put on my apron.

I was working on a replacement slat for a crib bed — an easy job, just a matter of cutting it to length and planing it smooth. It was a slow morning, normal for that time of year. I sold a few pieces of the pottery we take on consignment from a local artisan, and a couple of old medicine bottles. Just before lunch the bell tinkled again.

I brushed the wood shavings from my apron, drained the last of the latte and went into the showroom. Standing in the doorway, wiping her boots on the mat, was Raphaella.

3

She was wearing a red woolen Hudson's Bay coat and a floppy white tam. The cold air had raised a bit of color in her pale skin, seeming to darken the birthmark. She caught sight of me.

"Oh" was all she said.

I couldn't find my voice. I felt my neck and face flush hot, and something leapt in my stomach.

"I didn't know you worked here," she said, pulling off thick knitted mittens.

"Er, we own the place."

"Oh. Well, that's great."

Her eyes roamed the room. Mine stayed locked on her. How many love songs had I heard that said, "She takes my breath away"? Now I knew what that line meant. My legs were numb. My vocal cords didn't seem to work properly any more. I was painfully conscious of my stained apron and the block plane in my hand.

"You have some nice pieces here," she commented, running her hand along a maple sideboard.

"Thanks. Dad finds them."

"I wouldn't have figured you for the antique type," she said. "No offence."

"I refinished almost everything here," I blurted. "The furniture, I mean." I shut up before I made another stupid remark.

One corner of her mouth turned up in a half-smile. She touched a water jug and porcelain basin sitting on a pine dry sink, then traced the grain in the wood with her finger. "Nice work."

"Thanks. Um, can I help you with anything?"

"I hope so. You know, the OTG is putting on a musical at the beginning of the summer."

"Yeah, I heard something about it."

The Orillia Theatre Group put on plays and musicals regularly. Mostly musicals. I hate musicals, but I tried to look interested.

"We're doing *The Sound of Music.*"

Great, I thought. The musical I hated most. A cute governess who knows everything, nause-atingly cute kids, cute songs, a few Nazis who were so stupid you'd wonder why anybody was afraid of them. And nuns.

"I'll have to try and take it in," I said. If she was in it, I'd see it.

"Good. Well, the reason I'm here, I'm the stage manager, and the official props-gofer. I was hoping your store — you — might lend us a few pieces of furniture for the set."

If she'd asked for the deed to the store and everything in it I'd have handed them over, no questions asked. Briefly, I wondered if Dad would mind if I agreed to lend the OTG what they wanted. Freddy Graham at the bookstore occasionally borrowed stuff from us for his window displays. Then I had a thought.

"Tell you what," I said. "I'll lend you anything you want."

"Thank you. You're very —"

"On two conditions," I cut in, bolder now. What do I have to lose? I thought.

Raphaella smirked. "And they are?"

"One, you'll give us credit in the program. 'Antiques courtesy of,' something like that."

"Sure. We would have done that anyway." She waited. "And the second?"

"You'll have that cup of coffee with me."

That brought a deep laugh. She put a hand on her hip, arched her eyebrows. "I told you. I don't drink coffee."

Her words lacked the dismissive tone I had heard in my one disastrous phone call to her.

"Whatever you want, then. Herbal tea, hot chocolate, juice, milk, mineral water, ice cream, root beer, melted snow or —"

She laughed again. "Okay. Juice. Apple, if you have it."

"And," I said, "you have to promise not to call me Gannet any more."

"That's three conditions."

"I drive a hard bargain."

"Agreed. Garnet."

"Good. Wait here. Take off your coat and relax. I'll be right back."

A few minutes later I returned with two bottles of apple juice.

"Let's drink them back in the workshop," I suggested.

When she turned to walk where I pointed, I flipped the sign in the window around to read "Closed."

4

Raphaella took off her coat and draped it over the back of a rock maple dining-room chair. On her black T-shirt was printed "I Hate Banks."

"Who's Banks?" I asked.

"Not Banks, banks."

"Oh, I see, banks."

"Right, banks."

I took up my work again, just to keep my hands busy and give me something to do. I knew I'd fidget if I didn't.

"That's a beautiful crib," she said. "It's a cliché , I know, but they don't make them like that anymore."

"They can't. They're illegal, considered an unsafe design. But I know what you mean."

I removed the slat from the vise and ran a bit of sandpaper over it. I had already drilled and countersunk two holes in each end, so I fitted it into place and screwed it down tight. Raphaella watched every move, making me slightly self-conscious, as if she was memorizing each step.

When I put down the screwdriver and took a mouthful of juice, she said, "Are you sure you're the same guy who was praising logic and reason in the debate?"

"Why do you ask?"

"You love wood."

She was inviting me to share something I seldom talked about, except to my parents. Before I knew it, I was babbling away as if I'd known her for years. I told her about the pleasure and sense of achievement it gave me to fashion something from a piece of walnut or oak, how I sometimes felt a sort of communion with the wood, how, when I worked, I entered a state of concentration that dissolved my sense of time.

"That's why, when I'm here alone on Saturdays, I only do simple jobs like this one," I said. "If I get into a really complicated or delicate project, I lose track of everything else and forget to mind the store."

She laughed. "I'll bet you've lost a few sales that way."

"Dad got some complaints there for a while."

"Have you ever made a piece of furniture from scratch?"

"You mean copies?"

"I was thinking about originals."

How had she known that was exactly what I wanted to do? When I had time on my hands, mostly at school when the teacher droned on about land formations or family planning, I doodled and sketched cabinets, chests, tables — whatever came to mind, then balled up the paper and threw it away.

"I'm afraid to try, if you want to know the truth."

Raphaella made no reply.

"I'm scared that if I try I'll mess up and ruin everything. I sound like a coward, I know."

She shook her head, but still said nothing.

"My dream is to find someone to teach me to design furniture, then open my own shop one day. I don't care if I make a lot of money, just enough to get by and live the way I want."

"Then do it," she said simply, as if she was commenting on the weather.

I laughed self-consciously. "Yeah, all I have to do is convince my mother. She wants me to Be Somebody."

"I know the feeling," she said.

A little later, Raphaella looked at her watch and told me she had to go.

"I enjoyed our talk," she said at the door.

It was only after she had left that I realized she hadn't said a word about herself.

ς

Normally when I talked with girls, I couldn't relax. I believed that I had to say something clever or witty, or their attention would slip away. I'd make stupid jokes or end up saying something I didn't mean. And I often had the impression girls felt the same way, so there was a constant tension that ruined everything. I couldn't be who I was. I was always being judged, as if I had a meter attached to me that gave a reading somewhere between "cool" and "loser."

That afternoon, with Raphaella, it was completely different. Once I got over being rattled by her unexpected visit to the store, I talked like a normal human being. I wasn't constantly monitoring my words or mentally checking the loser meter.

What was it about her that had that effect on me? I didn't know, but I liked it.

chapter

That same spring my family had been thrown into turmoil by what Mom and I had taken to calling the house thing. It was a typical Gareth Havelock scenario. The Bertram House, a Victorian monstrosity on the corner of Brant and Matchedash Streets with a mansard roof, a wrought-iron fence enclosing the yard, old hardwood trees shading the property, had come up for sale. Dad had had his eye on it for years, dying to buy it, renovate it and fill it with antiques. Mom was almost as keen as he was. I wanted to stay where we were, the house I had grown up in, but nobody asked.

What should have been a simple real-estate deal — buy a house, sell the one you're in, arrange a moving day — fell apart. We sold our modern bungalow on Peter Street across from the golf links — Orillia had a small course right in town — but the buyers wanted to move in before we got legal possession of Bertram. There would be a "little gap," Dad told Mom and me. A gap of a couple of months. Probably. Unless the three parties could come to an arrangement.

We couldn't move into the apartment above the antique shop because the tenant had a lease. Besides, he was a family friend, a truck-parts sales-man who was on the road a lot. Enter another family friend who owned and operated a mobile home park, Silverwood Estates, west of town. We would store our furniture and live in a trailer. Great. A trailer. Three of us. Way to go, Dad.

As if things weren't crazy enough, Mom got a call from *National Scene* newsmagazine and, as she put it breathlessly when we were on the patio finishing a course of semi-burnt Dad-style hamburgers, the magazine made her an offer "I can't possibly turn down."

"*Now*, Annie?" Dad complained. "You want to go now, in the middle of things?"

Mom looked at me, to share her excitement, I guessed. She didn't see what she wanted.

"Now just a second, you two," she said. "Gareth, the things we're in the middle of are all your doing, so don't start playing that tune.

Besides," she added weakly, "there'll be more room in the trailer —"

"It's a mobile home."

"— with me gone."

"I think the hedge needs trimming," Dad said, getting up and heading for the shed at the foot of the yard.

Mom blew out a puff of air in exasperation. "You just trimmed it yesterday."

"Well, I missed a few spots," Dad mumbled.

"Where this time?" I asked Mom after a few minutes of uncomfortable silence.

The *snip*, *snip* of Dad's shears seemed louder than necessary.

Mom's eyes took on the excited twinkle she got when a trip was coming up. "East Timor," she said.

"East *where?*"

"Timor. East Timor. It's part — or was, until it voted for independence — of Indonesia, which wasn't happy about the vote and has been trying ever since to quash it with an underground campaign."

"And the magazine wants you to tramp right into the whole mess?"

Mom went on to explain that there was trouble in East Timor — again — and the U.N. was planning to send in a peacekeeping force — again. The magazine wanted her in place when the U.N. came in, to cover their arrival and the reaction of hostile, out-of-control militia groups, which were apparently sponsored by the Indonesian army.

"Sounds dangerous, Mom. Maybe you should reconsider."

"Oh, I'll be all right," Mom assured me. "I'm a tough old bird."

"It doesn't matter how tough you are and you know it," I said, my eyes on Dad's back as he attacked the hedge. "If it was safe there, there'd be no story and you wouldn't be going."

"I need to go," Mom said. "In this business you have to keep up your momentum. If you're off the pages for long, people forget about you."

"When do you leave?"

"In a couple of weeks."

"I hope you get back while we still have a hedge left," I said.

2

The day Raphaella had come to see me in the shop, I was, for once, in a pretty good mood when I came home after closing the store. Dad was in the kitchen, peeling potatoes.

"Hey, Dad," I greeted him, opening the fridge and taking out a can of pop.

"Hi, Garnet. Good day?"

"Not bad. Sold a few small things. Finished the crib." I didn't tell him the shop had been closed for a couple of hours.

"Fine," he said distractedly.

"Um, Dad," I began, sitting down at the kitchen table. "Would this be a good time to bring up my latest idea about school?"

He groaned, almost, not quite, silently. "I guess you told your mother about not going on past high school."

"Yeah."

"And?"

"About what you'd expect."

He washed the potatoes and cut them into chunks, put them in a pot of water and turned on the stove.

"So, what's the new idea?"

"Drop out now."

"*What*? You're almost finished. A month or two and you're out — with a diploma." Then he got that crafty look of his. "You want to pull this off *when* your mother's away, don't you?"

I dodged the question. "I can't stand school any more. I hate it and I don't need it. The bottom line is, it's my life. I ought to be able to make the decision."

He crossed his arms on his chest. He didn't look very firm, not wearing a sky-blue apron with big red chrysanthemums splashed all over it.

"If you go through with it, you've got to have a plan," he said.

Hooray! I almost shouted. He was weakening. "I do. I'll work at the store every afternoon and look for a cabinetmaker who wants an apprentice. I've also checked into a couple of community colleges that have courses in design."

He smiled. "You need your diploma to get into community college."

He thought he had me. "No, I don't," I said. "The courses are given at night, and there's no prerequisite."

"If you're out of school you need a job."

"I have a job. At the store."

"Well, that might not be enough, you know. Minimum wage, half a day, that's not much income."

"What do you mean?"

"What I mean is, quitting school has consequences. One of which is to earn enough to keep yourself. I'm not sure you qualify right now."

I began to see his strategy. He and Mom had obviously cooked all this up.

"So, let me get this straight," I said, staying calm, not letting my voice rise. "If I quit school I turn from a son into a tenant who lives at your house and eats your food. And I have to pay for that — room and board."

He nodded. Behind him, the potatoes began to bubble.

"And you're saying that I don't earn enough at the store to cover it."

He nodded again.

"Suppose I get another job, full time."

"Then you wouldn't be able to pursue your goal, would you? Not enough time." He turned down the heat under the pot and opened the oven door. Chicken wings sizzled away on a roasting pan.

"On the other hand . . ." Dad said, his back to me, letting his sentence trail off.

Here it comes, I thought. The net is about to fall on my head.

"If I stay in school," I finished his sentence, "and graduate, we can come to an arrangement."

Dad closed the oven door, removed a tossed salad and a bottle of dressing from the fridge, along with a bottle of Creemore Springs beer.

He uncapped the bottle and drank from it, then sat down at the table.

"Right. Now, here's the thing," he began. "I think we've got your mother onside about you not going to university. This has been hard for her. Don't think it hasn't. She had big hopes for you, but she's coming around. Still, dropping out of high school — that would break her heart. You owe her, Garnet. You've got to finish this thing properly, for her sake if not for yours."

I sat back in my chair, expelled my breath. "The laying on of guilt," I said. "Every parent's joy."

Dad smiled. "One of the few real pleasures in life."

He took another pull on the beer. "Want to hear the good news?"

"Sure," I said, letting my disappointment show. Putting it on display. I could do the guilt thing, too.

But Dad wasn't having any of that. He looked very pleased with himself.

"Okay, I've managed to get the house transaction straightened out."

Big deal, I thought. I don't want to move anyway.

"That's point one. Two, the mobile home we

were going to use is still available, and a little job comes with it. Roy Weeks is going away for a few months — he has family down in Arizona — and he wants someone on site at the park to act as superintendent. You mow the grass. That's about it. If someone has a problem, plumbing, septic tank or whatever, you call a repair shop from a list he'll leave you. He's willing to take you. You can live in the trailer, go to school, work at the store on Saturdays, keep an eye on things for him, earn a small wage. What do you say?"

I was confused. After blackmailing me into staying in school, he was talking about another job. "So you'll line this job up for me if I stay in school. And the reason I stay in school is, if I drop out, I need a job, which I don't have."

"For a gifted student, you can be a bit dim," he joked. "I've moved on from that, so try and follow. Roy needs a hand. I thought of you, that's all. It would give you a chance to save some money."

"Over the summer."

"Actually, he wants you to start right away. Now, want to hear part three?"

Feeling a bit over my head, I nodded.

"I've spoken to a fellow I used to do business

with, before you became Olde Gold's refinisher
and refurbisher. You've heard me mention him
— Norbert Armstrong over in Hillsdale."

Armstrong, I knew, was a master cabinet-
maker. I had planned to approach him about
taking me on as an apprentice. I looked Dad in
the eye and nodded.

"He's agreed — if you do — to accept you
in September, half days. That way you could
still work in the store and have time to take
your courses."

"Dad! You're kidding!"

"I'm not kidding."

"That's great!"

"But, my bonny lad, like all things in life,
this deal comes with a condition."

"Gee, I wonder what that is."

"So, you're staying in school."

"And loving the idea," I sneered.

"Don't look a gift horse in the mouth."

"I never did know what that meant."

"Well —"

"Never mind, Dad."

chapter

A week went by, a week of heavy homework and a major English essay on *Wuthering Heights*. Now there was a couple of strange ones, Cathy and Heathcliff, skulking around the windy moors under a brooding sky.

Raphaella turned up in English once, on Wednesday, but had slipped away after class before I could talk to her. I thought about her constantly, carried the ache around like a bulky package I was afraid to put down.

So that night I phoned her. The mother answered.

"It's the bird guy," she called out after I told her who I was. "Gannet."

"I'm *Gar*net," I corrected her hopelessly. "G-A-R —"

"Tell him you're busy or something."

"Hello."

"Hi, Raphaella. How are things?"

"Fine."

"Let's go to a movie tonight."

"I can't."

"Don't tell me. You have to wash your hair."

My lame attempt at a joke fell flat.

"No, I'm just busy."

"Tomorrow, then?"

"Sorry."

"I'd really like to see you again."

"I don't think that's a good idea."

"Are you going with someone?"

"No."

"Did I do something wrong?"

"No."

Wow, this is going well, I thought.

"Well, let's get together, then."

"Look, I'm sorry. I have to go."

"But —"

"Bye."

She wasn't in class next day or Friday. I began to wonder if she skipped off just to avoid me.

On Saturday morning a warm spring wind blustered up and down the sidewalk, rattling the budding branches of the trees along

Mississauga Street. I opened up the store at the usual time, got my coffee from next door — I needed it; I had hardly slept — turned the "Open" sign to face the street and put Beethoven on the CD player. The showroom looked a little bare — the theatre people had come by and picked up the pieces Raphaella had chosen for the set of *The Sound of Music* or, as I thought of it, *The Worst Musical Ever*.

I was a little on edge about Raphaella rejecting me and my complete failure to come up with a clever stratagem that would win her heart, or at least get her to talk to me, so I decided not to work out back that day. I selected an old leather-bound gilt-edged book from the shelves along the wall, settled into a re-upholstered loveseat with my coffee at hand, put my feet up on a 150-year-old needlepointed ottoman and opened the book. It was Edgar Allan Poe, just the thing to cheer me up.

"For the most wild, yet most homely narrative which I am about to pen, I neither expect nor solicit belief," began "The Black Cat," one of the few of his stories I hadn't read. "Mad indeed would I be to expect it." Great stuff, wild mystery, insanity, dark happenings. I sipped my coffee and slouched deeper into the soft seat.

The writing was gripping but I fell asleep anyway and sank into a nightmare. I was running through a night forest, panting with exhaustion and terror, pursued by a razor-clawed, slavering black cat with eyes like fire. Frantic, I pressed forward, but my legs wouldn't work, as if I was running waist-deep through mud. Behind me bounded the cat, ready to leap, sink its claws into my back and pull me down before tearing my flesh with its teeth.

The ground fell away and I floated like a falling leaf, landing in a grassy field that hissed at my legs as I stumbled along through the dark toward a building that loomed ahead. I pushed open the door to escape the cat, slammed it behind me. Shaking, I curled up on the floor in the corner.

Then I heard voices. Angry voices, heavy with fear and loathing, the words running together like distant thunder.

Eighty wish.

Now!

Go back!

No, no!

Stones, stones!

A bell rang in the distance and the voices drifted away like mist.

"Hey, Garnet."

I leapt from the loveseat, sending the book flying and upsetting the coffee, and stood trembling, blinking against the bright light in the window.

"Who's there?" I demanded.

When my eyes adjusted I recognized Brad Summerhill, whose father ran one of the local weekly auctions. He was wearing his usual bush shirt, jeans and broken-down high-tops, and he carried a clipboard in his right hand.

"Got a delivery for you," he said.

"Oh, okay," I managed, my heart hammering. "What is it?"

"Bunch of stuff your old man snagged at the Maitland sale."

"If you bring it around back to the usual place, that will be fine."

"You got to help me unload, though. The price only covers delivery."

Brad always carried a clipboard, always came through the front door rather than the back, always said the same thing.

"Sure, Brad. Glad to help."

"Long as you know."

"I know, Brad. I know."

chapter 10

By a strange — well, maybe not so strange — thought process, helping Brad unload Dad's latest haul brought me to Raphaella. I lugged a spinning wheel directly into the showroom, thinking it would partially fill the empty space made by the loan to the opera house, then looked across the street to the ugly old red-brick building itself. Was she there? Fifty yards away? Ignoring me?

By the time I had signed the waybill, thanked Brad and sent him on his way, Raphaella had taken over my mind like an invading army, and I was good and angry. Why had she dismissed me so abruptly on the phone? We had had a nice talk in the shop that day. She had seemed relaxed, friendly, not eager to get away. I was sure she wasn't being friendly because of the deal we had made about the furniture.

So why the brush-off?

Okay, she didn't want to go anywhere with me. Fine. But she could at least have told me why. Or at the minimum, she could have been polite. What was I, a leper?

The more I turned thoughts over in my head, the angrier I got.

I shrugged into my jacket, put the "Back in a minute" sign in the window, hastily locked up the store and stomped across the road. The stage door at the rear of the building was unlocked. I climbed a set of dimly lit stairs and found myself backstage in a confusion of chairs, dangling ropes, garment racks hung with old-fashioned gowns and morning coats, props of all kinds.

Voices coming through the curtains from front stage indicated that a rehearsal was in progress. When my eyes had adjusted to the gloom I caught sight of Raphaella on the other side of the backstage area, sitting in the glow of a small lamp, a headset on, a clipboard on her lap.

She was wearing black denims and a scarlet T-shirt that said "Tax the Rich." The lamplight fell on her bare arms and the curves of her upper body. Desire surged through me like an electric current, burning away my anger.

I approached quietly. Intent on her work, she didn't notice, but spoke softly into the mike and made a notation on her clipboard. Unselfconsciously, she reached up and tucked her hair behind her ear, revealing the birthmark, lending a trace of vulnerability to her beauty.

My heart pounded in my ears. My throat went dry. I whispered her name.

Calmly, she looked up, pressed her finger to her lips to signal quiet. She pointed to her watch, held up her hand with the fingers splayed, five minutes, and turned her attention to her notes.

I stood watching her, my resolve leaking away as each minute passed. What was I going to say to her, now that I'd dropped the idea of telling her off? How would I justify interrupting a rehearsal? Now she'll really think I'm a loser, I thought. A little puppy too stupid to realize he's not wanted.

"All right, everybody, that was fine," came a man's voice from the other side of the curtain. "Take ten and we'll do the third scene."

Raphaella stood up, her dark eyes sparkling in the lamplight. I figured I had about five seconds to persuade her to talk to me or she'd brush me off again. But I still couldn't think of what to say. I opened my mouth to speak.

But instead of talking I stepped toward her, took her in my arms and kissed her.

In an instant, thoughts darted through my mind.

Her lips are full and soft, just as I imagined.

Her hair and skin smell wonderful.

Her arms are hanging loose at her sides; she's not responding.

The small of her back is firm and slender.

Her lips aren't responding either.

The swell of her breasts burns against my chest. God.

I could be charged with sexual assault for this.

I flashed back to grade one and Evvie McFadden, the love object I had kicked in the shin.

But slowly, Raphaella's arms rose to embrace me, one hand behind my head. Her breathing quickened. I kissed her harder, then broke away.

"I know it sounds corny," I said hoarsely, "like I took the line from a bad movie, and you probably don't want to hear this, and —"

"Shut up and say it."

"I've loved you from the moment I saw you."

"But you don't believe in love at first sight, remember?" she whispered, and this time she kissed me, long and hard.

"Hey!" someone yelled from across the stage. "Are you guys gonna come up for air soon?"

2

"This," my father crowed triumphantly, "is not for sale." He held a bashed-up book with half the leather cover missing.

"Who'd want it? It's just an old book."

"It's more than that, kiddo."

"So?"

"Tell you later," he said, putting the book back into a box filled with other old volumes.

Dad and I were poring through the stuff he had bought at an auction on a farm out in Oro. I hardly paid attention to his excited ramblings. My every nerve still tingled from being with Raphaella a short time before. Our great love scene had drawn a few laughs and barbed comments from the cast of the *WME*, and Raphaella had sent me away, saying she'd talk to me as soon as rehearsal was over.

I was in shock, at the boldness of my action and — more — at her *re*action. Who would have guessed that, rather than scream "Rape!" or punch me or bite my lip in disgust, Raphaella would wrap her slender arms around me and squeeze as if she'd never let me go? I couldn't figure it out. And at that moment I didn't care.

My father was as churned up as I was, for a different reason. Strictly speaking, he hadn't participated in the auction at all. He had pre-empted it by contacting the Toronto lawyer handling the Maitland estate and offering a lump sum for the entire contents of the house. The remaining items — lawn tractors, patio furniture, two cars, some old farming equipment — went on sale to the public.

"He thought he was pulling a fast one on a country bumpkin awed by his big-city sophistication," Dad said, still going on about the lawyer. "He pulled up in his luxury SUV, wearing a Peak Outfitters parka, brand-new hiking boots, every inch the outdoors man from downtown, and talked to me as if I was a cretin. I played along, trying hard not to drool out the corner of my mouth or say 'aw shucks' while we worked out the deal."

All I knew of the Maitland farm was that it was old, one of the original pioneer homesteads in Oro going back to the early 1800s. According to Dad, who was up on all that stuff, the original farmhouse had been added to and refurbished over the years. The last surviving Maitland, who lived in California and had left the farm unused for two years after his mother died, finally put the whole place, chattels and all, up for sale.

Dad really had scored a big one this time. Along with a lot of junk there was furniture, some of it priceless, original paintings, silverware, lamps, carpets, blanket boxes — enough to keep Olde Gold Antiques and Collectibles stocked for a long time. The loot, as Dad called it, would keep me busy for another century, it seemed.

I set the boxes aside, mumbling that we had enough cracked-leather-bound Dickens and Thackeray and Haliburton and Susanna Moodie to outfit a geriatric library. But nothing could ruin my mood that day.

I had kissed Raphaella and she had kissed me back.

part TWO

chapter 11

For someone about to fly halfway around the world, my mother was traveling light. Aside from her laptop in its leather case and a roomy carryall, she had only one bag. The three pieces sat in the hallway by the front door.

Dad was teaching that morning and had already left the house. But, as usual when Mom was off on one of her career-enhancing jaunts, she and Dad had stayed up most of the night talking, drinking wine, putting off the dawn as long as they could. They'd had breakfast together and said their goodbyes before he left for work.

When she bounced down the stairs that morning in her usual traveling outfit — work shirt, jeans and leather moccasins — she looked more like a senior counsellor on her way to summer camp than a tough-minded journalist. But tough-minded or not, she seemed vulnerable to me, not at all equipped to dig out facts in a dangerous place. She hadn't left yet and I was already worried.

I hugged her tightly when the airport service mini-bus came to pick her up. "Be careful, Mom. Don't do anything dumb."

She kissed me and pulled the door open. "Okay, Gramps."

2

Moving day was, to use an oxymoron, a hectic bore. Dad had planned the whole operation like a military campaign. He went to the new house on Brant and I stayed at the old one. The movers loaded up the truck under my eyes and unloaded again under his.

I packed up my room — or some of it — and stowed my stuff in the van, because I was moving out to the mobile home, which I hadn't even seen yet. I was looking forward to living alone, but at the same time I was a little scared by the idea of being independent. I was also pretty sad about leaving the house I had grown up in.

Late in the afternoon, after the movers had driven off with the last load, I drifted from room to empty room, my footsteps echoing hollowly. The walls of the living and dining rooms had light oblongs on them where paintings had hung or furniture had stood against them. Dustballs lurked in corners. In the kitchen, cupboard doors hung open to reveal empty shelves.

All day I had been putting off this dark moment. My home was to be occupied by strangers. My mother was halfway around the world. My father would be buzzing around, humming cheerily in the house he'd waited years to buy.

I decided not to leave yet. I phoned Dad and told him my plans, then went out to the van to get the sleeping bag, recalling with a bit of a shiver the last time I had used it. I called out for a pizza, ate it in the family room, sitting on the floor, back against the wall, listening to tapes of old radio shows from Dad's collection: "The Shadow," "Inner Sanctum." Then I went to sleep.

I dreamed that I woke up with a fire in my belly, fueled by triple cheese and pepperoni — heartburn. At first I thought I had left the tape deck running. I reached over and pushed the power button. But the voices kept on. Voices I knew.

"Oh, no," I moaned. "No."

Eighty wish, I heard. *Eighty wish.*

chapter 12

I picked up Raphaella at the end of her street late the next morning after having breakfast with Dad at the new house. He was happy as a kid on Christmas morning.

"You're late," she said as she got into the van.

"Rough night."

"Oh?"

"A combination of too much pizza and a nightmare."

"So you're quoting Shakespeare to make you feel better."

"Ummm . . ."

"In *Macbeth*. The morning after he murdered Duncan and before Macduff and Lennox discovered the body. They're talking about storms and stuff, and Macbeth, who was half out of his mind with guilt and fear, says, ''Twas a rough night.'"

"Oh."

"It's kind of ironic. Understatement. Get it?"

"Moronic?"

"Ho, ho. You were also upset about leaving your old house for the last time."

Following Raphaella's train of thought wasn't always easy. In the short time we'd been together I had grown used to the feeling that sometimes came over me when I was with her — that she could read my mind. Or, to put it more accurately, she could read my feelings. Raphaella was like an antenna for emotions. I told her it was spooky. She said no, it was *intuitive*, and that people underestimated intuition.

"Yeah," I said. "I spent a long time chasing memories from room to room. It's funny, isn't it? After all, it's just a building."

"There are buildings and there are buildings," she said.

I drove west on Highway 12 where it skirts Orillia to the south. Buses lumbered past in the opposite direction, carrying gamblers to the casino in Rama at ten-thirty in the morning. I turned onto the Old Barrie Road. The sun was directly behind us and we chased our own shadow along the two-lane secondary road.

Raphaella was wearing loose cotton pants

and a T-shirt that said "Global Ecology Not Global Economy."

"Do all your T-shirts have captions on them?" I asked.

She smiled and pulled her hair back, looping an elastic band around it to make a long ponytail.

"I prefer them to corporation logos. Anyway, want to tell me about the nightmare?"

"It's a long story."

"Okay."

We drove in silence. In the distance the slanting sun illuminated the greening fields and the trees blushing with new buds. The road wound in gentle turns through the low hills.

Raphaella didn't press me about the dream. She didn't pry, ever. And she expected the same from me. There was still a lot I didn't know about her. Like who or where her father was. Where she and her mother had come from — they'd been in Orillia for only three years. Why she had transfered from Park Street Collegiate in the middle of the semester.

What I did know was that she lived on Couchiching Point in a house on the canal. Her mother preferred to live on the water, Raphaella had said, typically refusing to elaborate. Her mother owned and operated the Demeter health food store in town, where Raphaella worked in her spare time — which she had lots of, because she was a half-time student. That was about it.

I was curious, but I didn't press things. If she wanted me to know she'd tell me, I'd learned. If she didn't, there was no way to pry anything out of her. That was okay with me. I was in love with her, not her family or her background.

"So, where's this trailer park, anyway?" Raphaella asked.

"Do you mind?" I said in a mock British accent. "One doesn't say trailer park. One says mobile home estate." Then, in my normal voice, "It's on the Third Concession Line."

"Ah, yes," Raphaella intoned. "An enviable address indeed. Just past the bustling metropolis of Edgar, I believe."

I laughed. As she spoke, we were passing through Edgar, a four-corner nowhere village with one store.

"That's the Third Concession up ahead," I pointed out. "We go left."

A lone building at the crossroads came into view.

"We'll, I'll be —"

It looked different in bright spring sunshine. The large windows were trimmed in white that contrasted sharply with the dark plank walls. The lilac bush by the door was in bud. When I turned off the paved road onto the gravel concession line, I saw the stone and mortar structure. The one I had crashed into.

"Yup, that's it, all right," I said to myself.

"Why are we stopping?" Raphaella asked. "And what's what?"

"That's the church where I spent the night last March. Remember? I told you about getting trapped there in the blizzard." I hadn't told her about the dream. "Let's take a look," I said.

We crossed the road. Sure enough, the stones were chipped and there were faint traces of blue paint on the mortar.

"It's some kind of monument," Raphaella said, her voice uneasy. "Look."

On the side opposite the one I'd hit was a bronze plaque that told us that the African Methodist Church had been built in 1849. Below the notation was a list of those "who worshipped and are buried here."

"African?" I said. "I don't get it."

Rural Ontario was a long way from Africa.

And you could count the black families in the area on one hand.

I looked around. "There aren't any gravestones. So where are the graves?"

Around the church, the grounds were grass-covered. About thirty yards away was a forest of maple trees.

"I guess the grassy part is the cemetery. Come on," I suggested. "Let's look inside."

"Maybe I'll wait in the van," Raphaella said quietly.

"Just a quick look, then we'll go."

I soon regretted my decision. Like dampness from cold stone, the church gave off an atmosphere of dread that I could feel on my skin and in my bones. Determined not to give in to my uneasiness, I pushed on. It's a sunny spring day, I told myself. Birds are chirping in the trees. This isn't Castle Dracula.

I led Raphaella along the side of the church and looked in the windows, recalling the fright I had had that night when I had thought I'd seen a man watching me. Inside, the place appeared as I had left it. The benches that had been my bed stood before the stove.

"Look," I said to Raphaella, "you can see

where the original logs have been covered with siding. And there's —"

Her face was ashen, and she held her hands at her waist, fingers interlocked, knuckles white.

"What's the matter?"

"There are spirits here," she whispered, her eyes wide.

"What? How do —?"

"Something bad happened around here somewhere. Something evil. Garnet, please, let's go."

She clutched my arm as we walked back to the van. Which of us was more scared I didn't know.

chapter 13

The mobile home park was about five hundred yards down the road on the left, almost hidden from view by a row of tall cedars. I drove under an arch with "Silverwood Estates" printed across a rising-sun motif and followed a winding blacktop track, slowing for the speed bumps, until I came to an egg-yellow modular unit with a sign saying "Office" nailed to a deck post. I got a set of keys and Roy Weeks's handwritten instructions from the mailbox and we drove farther into the estate, looking for unit 99. I missed it the first time by.

"That's it," Raphaella pointed. "The one back there by itself, against the trees."

I reversed the van and drove up a dirt track to my new abode, a "single-wide" mobile home, pea green with white trim around the windows and door. A satellite dish sat on the roof. A wooden deck ran the length of the trailer. On three sides a lawn enveloped last year's flower gardens. We sat in the van, looking the place over. It would be private, and pretty quiet, I guessed, tucked up against the forest, separated from the other units.

Inside, it was bright, clean and almost new. The door opened into a little living room. Then there was a galley kitchen, bathroom and shower, and a good-sized bedroom at the back. Perfect.

I stowed my gear in the bedroom. A window looked out across a small patio to where a barbecue stood under a plastic tarp.

"Nice, eh?" I said to Raphaella from the bedroom.

She was leaning against the countertop. "Yeah, great."

Her face was still a little drawn, her voice edged with uncertainty. "How far away is that church?" she asked.

"About half a mile. There's a forest between here and there."

"Good."

I returned to the van and brought in the four bags of groceries we'd picked up in town.

Raphaella was opening windows when I came in.

We listened to music and talked for a while, arguing good-naturedly about whose CDs to play. Most of mine were either classical or jazz from twenty or thirty years ago. Raphaella had pop and — ugh — show tunes.

"As long as I don't have to listen to the *WME*," I complained, and Raphaella threw a dish towel at me.

We compromised, alternating hers then mine while we sipped cola (me) or juice (her). By mutual but unstated agreement, we avoided any mention of the church. Mostly, we talked about school, which Raphaella attended "casually," as she put it, meaning at most two days a week. She knew about the deal I had made with my father.

"What are you planning to do after graduation?" I asked. "College? University?"

"Oh, my future was decided before I was born."

When she didn't continue I urged, "Come on. You can't say something mysterious like that and let it drop. It's not fair."

"I'm supposed to operate a health food store. Like my mother."

"You don't sound too enthusiastic."

"And she expects me to follow in her footsteps — she's big on family history and tradition — and become a midwife."

That one threw me. "Is that a, um, profession?"

"Certainly it is. Midwives are recognized almost everywhere. Lots of women won't have their babies without one. The irritating thing is, I *am* interested in the things Mom wants, but it's not enough. I want to learn more about people, about psychology. I'm interested in why people act the way they do, and why they believe the things they do. Know what I mean?"

"Yeah."

"Mom's afraid that if I go to university and I'm away from home for a few years, I'll abandon her big plans for me. She keeps throwing that whole Park Street thing in my face whenever I talk about it."

This time, when Raphaella paused, I kept silent. Without my urging, she went on.

"You probably heard some things about me," she said.

"Just gossip. You know how it is."

"What did your hear?"

"Well, something about witches and stuff."

"I might have guessed. It was stupid. I did a seminar on the occult for history class — at least, some of it. It's a vast field. I concentrated on Wicca and Voudon, conjuring, spells, exorcism, stuff like that."

She said it casually, as if she was discussing different brands of toothpaste.

"You know what idiots people can be. After the seminar, rumors started to spread. I was a witch. I was a satanist. I'd find notes taped to my locker or hear remarks in the halls — never to my face, of course. Why would anyone think that because I did research on the occult that I buy into it all? It's not *what* people believe that fascinates me, it's *why* they believe it."

"So you don't swallow any of it."

"I didn't say that. Anyway, it all got so stupid that I decided to transfer to O. D."

"What about your father?" I asked. "Does he go along with your mother?"

She opened the door a crack, then shut it again. "Don't have one."

"He died?"

"No." Her voice tightened, warning me off.

"Divorce?"

"No. Hey, didn't you promise me a gourmet dinner?"

I let it drop. Maybe Raphaella's mom had gotten pregnant when she was single and the guy had taken off. That kind of thing wasn't exactly rare.

I put water on to boil for pasta and took vegetables from the fridge.

"I'll watch," Raphaella said. "You can teach me how to cook. I can't boil water without burning it."

"Old joke. Old bad joke. You sound like my father."

When the water was rolling, I put in the spaghetti. I peeled an onion, squinting against the tears as I chopped it in half and then sliced thin half-moons off each half. Next I cut florets off a stalk of broccoli.

"Do you like garlic? I forgot to ask."

"Yes."

"There's only one rule about cooking with garlic," I said as Raphaella began to set the table. "You put it in everything."

I peeled three fat cloves and chopped them up fine, then grated Parmesan cheese into a small bowl. I put a wide skillet on the stove over a medium heat and when it was hot, poured in olive oil, adding the onion, then the garlic. Immediately, a sweet, savory aroma filled the small kitchen. I tossed the ingredients slowly in the skillet, earning applause from Raphaella. I put in the broccoli, followed a few moments later by the pasta.

Raphaella stood next to me with her arm around my waist. "You're frying the spaghetti?"

"Not frying," I said, tossing the ingredients with a pair of tongs. "Sautéing. Only barbarians fry their food."

"Oh, excuse me. And what does sauté mean, may I ask?"

"Don't be technical."

I transferred the pasta to two bowls and put them on the table, and we sat down to eat. It was Raphaella who raised the subject first. "Tell me about that place," she said.

"Have you ever been there before?"

"No. Never heard of it."

"You seemed to, well, know something — from the way you reacted, I mean. Your face went pale."

"How could *my* face go pale?" she joked. "No, I've never been there. But the aura of the place is almost physical."

"And scary."

"Terrifying."

I nodded. "That makes me feel better. I was beginning to think I was a bit nuts."

We ate in silence for a few minutes.

Then I asked, "Are you bothered by grave-yards in general?"

Raphaella shook her head. "Not in the least."

"So it was that place, the African church, in particular."

"Yes."

"Well, I've got something to tell you."

I recounted my nightmare, leaving nothing out. Raphaella reacted as if I'd read her a grocery list. She paid close attention, kept her eyes on me as I talked, but she was completely calm, as if she heard stories like mine every day.

"And you've had this dream again?" she asked when I had finished.

"Yup. Once at the store and once at home — last night."

"Hmm."

"Exactly. And it scares the hell out of me. I wake up shaking and gasping for breath."

"I like that about you."

"Er, what?"

"That you're willing to admit you're scared."

"I wish I could say I wasn't. You said back at the church that there were spirits there. What did you mean? Ghosts?"

"Not ghost-story spooks. Not movie ghosts.

Presences. You know, some places are just creepy."

"But that's because our imaginations are working overtime. Like in a dark attic or basement in an old house. Whistling-in-the-dark stuff. You seem to be saying that there's really something there, at the church."

Raphaella took a deep breath. Her eyes strayed to the window and she seemed to be making a decision. "Yes," she said.

"You believe in these spirits or presences, or whatever."

"I think that there are reverent places, just like there are peaceful or beautiful or restful places."

"And evil places."

She nodded. "Yes. But not because there's a troll under the bridge or a dragon in the cave. Because of events that went on there."

"Wow," I said.

"Yeah, I know."

"I'm not making fun of you."

"I know."

Raphaella had given me her trust, shared something that, in another place, with other people, would bring ridicule down on her like a thundershower. We both knew that what we were talking about wasn't a clown in a sewerpipe, like in the King novel, or a few thirteen-year-olds charged with manufactured excitement tittering over a Ouija board.

"When we walk around," she said, choosing her words, working things out, "we leave our scent behind. It's — to us — invisible, odorless. We're not even aware of it. But a dog can track a human through a forest days after he passed by. And I've read that female moths give off whatchamacallits, phonemes —"

"Pheromones. Phonemes are —"

"Whatever. A few parts per million of those — things — and male moths can pick up the smell, the message if you want to call it that, from miles away."

"But that's a *physical* thing. You figure that, what, after we die something remains behind? What you call a presence?"

"I can't really explain it. But, well, I've never been to one of those Nazi concentration camps in Europe, the ones with the ovens, but I'm sure I'd feel the presence of the dead — the children and their parents and grandparents. They say that's true of old battlefields, too."

"Not very scientific," I said.

"No, but that doesn't mean much."

I got up from the table and put on the kettle for tea. Raphaella had brought me a few boxes of herbal teas of different flavors and blends, some fruity, others medicinal.

I glanced around my new place, at the stereo set in the living room, the little TV hooked up to a dish that pulled signals out of the air and descrambled them, at the telephone. High-tech, modern equipment. And here we were talking about spirits, whatever word we used.

"Do you think everybody who passes that old church gets the shivers?" I asked, using one of my father's old expressions.

"No. Definitely not. Some people are more sensitive, the way a radio tunes in to a particular station. People like you and me," she added, smiling.

"Lucky us," I said.

We did the dishes and then I drove Raphaella home. Up until then, she would get out of the van a block or so away from where she lived, but to my surprise she directed me right to her house, a bungalow with a big silver birch on the front lawn. I got the impression she was making a statement, pushing things a little with her mother. When I pulled into the driveway I noticed a slender woman in the picture window, hands on her hips, looking at us. Even from that distance the scowl on her face was visible.

"Uh-oh," Raphaella said in mock alarm. "The riot squad is waiting."

"She looks peeved," I said.

"You don't know the half of it."

"Is it me, or males in general?"

"In general. She doesn't want me to see anyone."

"She's training you to be a nun?"

"Dating isn't part of the plan."

"So she's been like this with all the boys you've —"

"Yup."

She planted a quick kiss on my mouth and jumped out of the van. As she walked up the flagstone path to her front door I plastered a smile on my face and waved at her mother. Garnet the smoothie.

She didn't return the wave.

2

Back at the trailer, I turned on the miniature TV in the bedroom and took a shower, banging my elbows on the walls of the cramped shower stall, before pulling on my PJs and crawling under the blankets. I flipped through the channels looking for a movie, but had to settle for a courtroom drama.

On most evenings, before I fall asleep, I go over the day in my mind, reliving conversations, second-guessing things I had said or done, hoping I hadn't made a fool of myself.

But not tonight. I wanted no rehash of Raphaella's speculations about the church. That whole topic was something to put aside, for a long time, if not for ever.

At some time during the cross-examination of the hero, I fell asleep. I drowsed fitfully, then woke again. The tiny bedroom pulsed and flickered with bluish TV light. On the screen, two long-haired Spandex-clad women with sincere looks and too much make-up were pitching exercise equipment. I used the remote to turn off the set and got a glass of water at the kitchen sink. The trailer was stuffy and warm. I opened the bedroom window a few inches and damp, cool, sweet-smelling air poured in. The rhythmic *chee-eep* of crickets came with it. A dog barked. I climbed back into bed, rolled over and dozed off.

This time I woke with a start, my eyes a foot from the illuminated numbers on the clock radio beside the bed: 12:00 A.M. The wind sighed in the bush behind the trailer. And then I heard what had awakened me.

A woman was crying, deep, urgent sobs fading in and out with the wind.

I hopped out of bed, turned on the light and ran to the door. Was it a domestic quarrel? Or partiers? I stepped outside into the cool, clammy air, wondering if there was 911 service this far away from town. I looked down the lane toward the cluster of mobile homes hidden behind evergreens. A few porch lights twinkled as the wind moved the spruce branches. I stepped out onto the path beside the van, arms crossed on my chest against the chill, ears cocked for human sounds. Nothing.

I went back inside. I locked the door this time, and leaving the outside light on, padded into the bedroom. I got back into bed and turned out the light.

The weeping returned, a profound, unearthly wail, rising and falling that made my skin crawl. I lay there, wondering who lived back there in the trees, because it was clear now that she was not in the trailer park. Lifted by the wind, the voice seemed to approach then pass by. Then it faded and was gone.

I punched up the pillows behind me and opened my book. I read for a while, until my eyes grew heavy, and the novel slid from my hands.

The clock read 3:00 A.M. when I heard her again, the same woman.

Help! she wailed. *Joo-ball, help me!*

Earlier, her cries had been enough to turn me cold, to creep into me like a damp chill.

Now she called out in terror several times —
Joo-ball, help me! — before her voice faded,
leaving only the wind.

I picked up the phone, keyed in the emergency number. Nothing but an irritating elec-
tronic voice telling me I hadn't put in enough
numbers. Should I call the cops? I wondered.
The night was quiet again. Maybe I hadn't
really heard anything. It was my first night in a
strange place. Maybe it had been the wind. I
imagined myself standing in the driveway, a
cop car with lights blipping on the roof, neigh-
bors in PJs and housecoats gawking while I
pointed into the forest, telling a cop I had heard
a woman there.

I decided to wait.

While I was waiting I fell asleep again.

3

In the morning, leaving for school, I saw a man
on his knees in a patch of cleared ground beside
his modular home, working the soil with a
hand cultivator. Green shoots peeked out of the
dirt in plant flats arranged around him. When
I got out of the van, he looked up, wiping his
brow on his sleeve.

"Morning," I said.

"How are you today?"

"Fine, thanks. I'm Garnet Havelock, just moved into the unit back by the trees."

"Yeah, Roy told me you'd be along. My name's Trevor."

"Nice to meet you. Sorry to interrupt your work."

"Oh, that's okay."

He was in his fifties, I guessed, tall and fit, a bit of grey at his temples.

"I was wondering," I began, "is there a house out there in the bush behind my trailer?"

"No, nothin' there but trees."

"I thought I heard somebody last night. A woman calling."

"Strange," he said. "I didn't hear anything myself. 'Course, Laura and me're heavy sleepers."

"Maybe someone was lost or something."

"Nobody goes back there," Trevor said, the friendly tone leaving his voice. "That's all Maitland land."

"Oh, well," I said, taken aback by his abruptness. "Probably just the wind."

He nodded. "Musta been. Nobody goes back there."

chapter

Trevor was wrong. That night I heard her again, coming and going. At midnight she passed by going north, uttering the same heart-wrenching sobs. Hours later, she returned, going south, crying out for help and raising the hair on the back of my neck.

In the morning I had a quick coffee, laced on my hiking boots and walked into the trees. The open bush was brushed with the vivid green of new, unfurled leaves, and thousands of trilliums speckled the forest floor with white. Last year's fall of leaves rustled softly underfoot. Squirrels skittered here and there, to and fro, and the air was alive with birdsong.

Soon I came across a path leading north and south. I was no woodsman, but I could tell it was not well traveled.

I elected to go left. After a hundred yards or so the terrain sloped, and spruce and cedar stood green against the grey trunks of the hardwoods. The ground underfoot was damp. I came upon a creek that intersected the path. A thick log that had fallen long ago formed a bridge across the stream. The moss on the log was undisturbed. I stepped along it carefully. After ten minutes I saw a clearing through the trees, and a small building. At the edge of the clearing, by a rail fence, I had an unrestricted view of green grass, a stone monument, and the African Methodist Church, lit by the slanting rays of morning sunlight.

I retraced my route, this time going past the spot where I had started following the path. The trail rose and fell with the terrain, twisting through the bush for about half a mile before turning into the sun. I climbed a steep hill and found myself at the edge of a small clearing, and I stopped.

I remained still, as if something had commanded me to stand unmoving. I scanned the clearing. It was carpeted with long dry grass and weeds. On one side a jumble of fallen and rotted logs enclosed the remains of a stone chimney. There was a strangeness about the place. An otherness.

On the edges of the clearing, branches stirred in the breeze, but the grass in the open area stood as motionless as it would on a sultry, windless July day, as still as a photograph. No birds flitted or soared overhead. No squirrel scampered across the ground.

And another thing. The ruin of decayed logs and mossy stones had fallen down long ago, but the surrounding forest had not reclaimed the open land. Not so much as a sapling grew there.

I took a breath and walked into the zone to the ruins of what had probably been a small cabin. It seemed a peaceful place, bathed in the yellow light of the morning sun, but there was a pervading chill there, a creeping, unwelcoming cold.

I wondered what Raphaella would think of the place. I decided to take her there.

2

It was late morning when I pulled into the driveway of our new house on Brant Street and parked in front of the detached double garage. It was run down, paint peeling off the ship-lap siding, shingles missing, and would need a lot of work. Just the thing Dad liked.

I walked around to the front of the house and onto the wide verandah and let myself in the front door. He was still at work, teaching music to the mites. I cruised the rooms, taking my time, noting the high ceilings, the wide baseboards and trim, the hardwood floors that creaked underfoot, the huge brick fireplace in the living room with the carved oak mantel. Inside, the place was in good shape. I could see why Mom and Dad had been so taken with it.

In the big kitchen at the back of the house I made some coffee and toast, and rummaged through the pile of newspapers Dad had left on the table. He'd clipped Mom's first two articles. I read them, not at all happy about what I learned.

East Timor, she wrote, was in a real mess. Militia groups, mostly teenage boys with guns, roved at will, killing anyone they thought supported home rule. It looked like civil war might break out if the U.N. couldn't keep both sides from each other's throats. Many of the locals were heading for the hills — literally. Added to that was religious strife. Christian and Moslem. Some of the militia were ultraconservative Moslems who tried to enforce very strict Islamic rules, Mom had written. Her disapproval of their treatment of women was pretty obvious.

I stacked the papers again and put my cup and plate into the sink. I climbed the stairs from the kitchen to the second floor — they were narrow and steep and there was a half-moon depression worn into each one — walked down the hall and took the stairs to the third floor.

Here, everything was more compressed, built on a smaller scale. There were two wainscotted rooms. The one at the front of the house had a door that let onto a small balcony with a wrought-iron railing. From the balcony I could see Lake Couchiching. This, I decided, would be my bedroom. I only had to convince Mom and Dad.

Downstairs again, I picked up the phone. Luckily, Raphaella answered.

"I've got something I want to show you out at Silverwood," I said mysteriously. "You're not going to school today, are you?"

"Forget it, Garnet. Mom's giving me a hard time. I have to lie low for a while. I'm working in the store today."

"What's her problem?"

"I told you. She doesn't want me seeing anyone."

"The plan you told me about."

"Yeah. Listen, Garnet, you'd better not call here any more. It just makes things worse."

My stomach fell. "Does this mean . . . Are you telling me . . . ?"

"No, no. I just mean you have to let *me* call *you*. I should be able to sneak out tomorrow."

"Okay," I said, relieved. "But at least let me tell you about what I —"

"Uh-oh. Got to go." And she hung up.

chapter 16

I went to school in the afternoon, sat through two classes that were so tedious my brain turned to cement, and headed for the Olde Gold. Dad was in the office, bent over a ledger.

"Hi, Dad."

"Hi, kiddo. What's new?"

"Not much."

"How're the new digs?"

"Digs?"

"Your place at Silverwood."

I made up some stuff about how peaceful it was out there, then I asked if he'd heard from Mom.

"Yeah, she called yesterday morning. Said she was trekking inland with a camera and another pen in a jeep to find some of the refugees. She says hi."

The way Dad talked, there were no people with Mom — just pens and cameras and tape recorders. Mom was a pen, too. He tried to make light of things, but I could tell he was worried.

I spent the next few hours taking inventory of all the loot from the Maitland estate, noting what should be cleaned and polished, refinished or repaired. Then I wrote up a schedule that prioritized the work. I showed the schedule to Dad.

"Great work," he said. "Let me take a closer look at it tomorrow. Right now, what say we put on the old feed bag at the Chinese buffet?"

I figured he meant dinner. "Sounds good," I said.

"Okay. Let's pull up stakes, podnah."

"Let's do that."

2

We caught a movie after we had eaten — a remake of a movie from the fifties that had been based on a play written in the thirties — and I dropped Dad off at the house and headed out to the trailer. Once inside, I put on a Bill Evans CD and read for a while in the living room. It was hard to concentrate, though, with my mind jumping from the crying woman to Raphaella, to the men in my dreams and back to Raphaella again.

What was her mother's problem? I wondered. I had met lots of controlling parents, but she turned overprotectiveness into sheer paranoia. Did she expect Raphaella to ignore males for the rest of her life? The more I thought about it, the less sense it made. She seemed to want Raphaella under her thumb, yet Raphaella was working on the musical with OTG. I had nothing against theater types, but some of them weren't the most conventional people in the world. And most protective parents were strict about attendance at school. Raphaella came and went as she pleased.

Maybe it was some sort of religious thing. There were lots of brands of religion in Orillia — statistically, we had a church for every two thousand people — and a few of them were pretty extreme. Raphaella hadn't mentioned anything about her mother's religion, but then again, she was close-mouthed about all family matters. She herself had never struck me as religious. Spiritual, yes, but not a rule follower. I concluded, not for the first time, that figuring out what made people tick wasn't one of my strong points.

About eleven o'clock I put my book down, turned off the CD and called it a night. A soft spring rain began to fall just as I was crawling between the sheets. I lay there listening to it hissing on the flagstones of the patio, thinking about dreams. The nightmare with the men's voices had scared me, but not in any deep, bottom-of-the-soul way, I reassured myself, not enough to make me afraid to sleep. And the woman calling and crying, well, that was not much more than a nagging mystery. It wasn't exactly an added attraction for the neighborhood, but it seemed no one else in the park could hear it, so maybe it was a freak noise produced by the wind. That was probably the explanation.

That was how I reasoned things through just before I fell asleep, and I didn't really believe a word of it.

3

I heard her at the usual time. At first, all I could make out over the hiss of the rain was a low moan, then I heard crying, faint but unmistakable, then only the rain. I decided to run a test. I set the clock radio for three-fifteen and went to sleep again.

Music woke me. Piano music, Liszt, on "Late Night Classics." In the background the roar of heavy ran. I dressed quickly, grabbed a flashlight and an umbrella and stepped out onto the deck. It was a warm rain, falling straight and hard through the still air, bouncing off the planks and splashing my calves. I walked to the edge of the trees and stopped. A curtain of water poured off the edge of the umbrella. I checked my watch: 3:25.

Logic dictated that I shouldn't hear anything above the rain. But, to my left, someone was panting heavily, as if running in full flight, each sobbing breath like a saw rasping back and forth.

Joo-ball! The word was torn from a throat gasping for breath. *Joo-ball, help me!*

She passed me quickly this time. I heard only her panicked gasps, no footfalls thumping on sodden ground. But her fear set my blood thundering in my ears.

Forcing myself to move, I took several steps forward into the bush and heard something that froze my blood.

Deep in the trees, the voices of men, angry, afraid, as if arguing. They were moving fast, their words like nails pounded into my skull. I held my breath, knowing what would come.

Eighty wish!
Go back!
No!

The men passed me, voices in violent conflict. And then, from farther away in the bush,
Help meeeee!

Her cry rose above the roar of the rain.

"You look awful."

"Thanks very much for the compliment."

"Like death warmed over."

"You're too kind."

"Like the 'before' segment of a sedative commercial."

"I get the point."

"When was the last time you got a decent night's sleep?"

"Can't remember. If I didn't have you to talk to, I think I'd go insane."

Raphaella smiled and tossed her hair over her shoulder. She was wearing a midnight blue T-shirt and a charcoal grey skirt that brushed the toes of her granny boots. The T-shirt read "Smoking Causes Profits."

We were in the office of the store, where I

had been making a catalogue of the books from the Maitland home when Raphaella dropped in after the Saturday-morning rehearsal of the *WME*, carrying take-out from the fish-and-chip restaurant down the street. Empty food cartons and juice bottles littered the desk.

"There's something else," I said, with hesitation.

Raphaella sat back in her chair, crossed her legs and gnawed at a fingernail. "Don't tell me. The woman you love is too secretive."

"Well, that's for sure, but it's not what I meant." Haltingly, I told Raphaella about the woman in the forest, not sure how to relate the story without sounding like a hysterical airhead in a Hollywood horror flick.

"She's been there every night?"

"Yup. At midnight and at 3 A.M. And now she has company."

I related to her what I'd experienced for the past few days, how the men in my dream had become part of the . . . ritual, or whatever was going on. Raphaella heard me out without a word, her head tilted to one side, her deep, intelligent eyes fixed on mine.

"Wow," she said when I finished.

"Exactly. I think I've gone over the edge."

"No, you haven't," she said firmly. "I've been out there, remember?"

"So what do you think?"

"I think, Mr. Garnet Havelock, that what you have on your hands is a first-class haunting."

2

A while later we were walking hand in hand in Tudhope Park, along the edge of the lake away from the main beach. Two toddlers stood in the shallows with their mother, tossing bits of bread to a family of ducks, while farther out the father hurled a stick for a golden retriever. The afternoon sun blazed down on us, and a cool breeze blew in off the lake.

We sat on top of a picnic table, looking past old willows with twisted, gnarled trunks out over the green rippled water where a few powerboats churned lines of white foam behind them.

"So, what do I do?" I asked finally.

"What we do," Raphaella replied, "is go back into the past. Find out all we can about that maple forest."

"And the clearing and ruined cabin. The one you haven't seen yet."

"Right. You said it was a weird place and

that the woman seems to start and end her walk in that area."

"It's weird, all right. As if the little clearing has its own weather."

"What is it that she calls out night after night?"

"The first word sounds like 'joo-ball' and then she says 'Help me.'"

"Well, that's easy. Jubal is a man's name."

The trouble with hanging around with sharp people is that every once in a while they make you feel stupid. Jubal. Help me, Jubal. Why hadn't I thought of that?

"Right," I agreed, pretending I had come to the same conclusion myself.

"Jubal means 'he who makes music,' or something like that," Raphaella said.

"How do —?"

"I've studied names and their meanings. Also numerology. Sort of a hobby."

"A hob —"

"Never mind. Your name means 'red jewel,' in case you didn't know."

"And yours?"

"Divine healer. Anyway, we have to go back into the past. Learn stuff. Find out who the woman is. It might be fun," she said unconvincingly.

"Yeah. And you know what else I want to do? Wait for her. In the bush. *See* her. But it might be dangerous, especially if I bumped into those men . . ."

One of the little kids shrieked with joy when the dog bounded into the lake in a shower of water, scattering the ducks in a chorus of angry quacks. Suddenly I felt ridiculous. There we were, calmly discussing ghosts. Or presences, as Raphaella would insist.

"There shouldn't be any danger, Garnet. Spirits from the past don't hurt you. Physically, I mean. They're, well, sort or re- enacting something, whatever it is that keeps them walking."

"I think I'd like to try to see her."

"Okay, let's do it."

"You'll come?"

"Yes. In the meantime, Sherlock Havelock, we've got some research to do."

3

"This is crazy," I complained. "How could I let you talk me into this?"

We were stopped at a red light near the Stephen Leacock Museum, just down the road from Tudhope Park, and I was having second thoughts. A bad case.

"Into what?" Raphaella asked, kicking off her sandals. She plunked her feet onto the dashboard and tucked her skirt around her legs.

I shook my head, disgusted with myself. "I think the stress is getting to me — Mom being away, moving out of my house, the stupid dream. And you've got me believing in ghosts."

"Spirits." There was an edge to her voice.

"Whatever."

"And people can't *make* you believe in something."

The light changed and I pulled away. "But it's nuts," I said. "It's the twenty-first century, the third millennium, two thousand and —"

"I know how to count, Garnet."

"What we've been talking about all morning only happens in books and movies."

"You're slipping into techno-mode."

"Into what?"

"Techno-mode. The attitude that science can explain everything, that computers and machines can solve all our problems. You sound like that physics teacher, What's-his-name, the one whose classes I never go to."

"Canelli."

"Right. 'Seeing is believing.' 'There must be a scientific explanation.' That whole complex."

"Yeah, well, I may be in techno-mode but I'm not too happy about the alternative view of the universe."

"The alternative is there whether you like it or not."

chapter 18

Raphaella had to work at her mother's shop for a few hours, so I hit the grocery store before heading to the house. Once there, I chopped up some fresh veggies for a stir-fry and put them in the fridge. I put a block of tofu in some marinade, and settled down in the family room to wait for Dad to get home from the store.

There were times when I thought I would have made a good candidate for one of those corny stories about split personalities. Except in my case I didn't have more than one person living in my head. I had only me, but I seemed to have two halves.

Raphaella was right. I was a digital junkie, a techno-mode person. I liked electronics with lots of lights and buttons on them, TV with loads of features, computer software — some of it — the whole modern thing. I didn't believe in statues that cry, Saturday-morning evangelists who heal cancer patients by touching them and shouting towards the ceiling, angels who brought messages from the beyond. Superstitions made me laugh.

On the other hand, I could never — all my life — shake the notion that there was more. There were things in life that couldn't be explained or measured. When I worked with wood, there was more to it than the mechanics of cutting and sanding and painting, something creative that I couldn't explain to someone even if I wanted to. And the way I felt about Raphaella, or the love between my parents, how to measure that, or figure it out? Love wasn't material. You couldn't go down to the Farmers' Market behind the library on Saturday morning and buy a pound of it. Love was spiritual.

There seemed to be no answer to this whole ghost business. It sounded crazy, but it wasn't crazy. All I could do was go by my experience, and I knew with the certainty of a headache or a burned finger that the voices I had heard in the forest at night were real.

2

Raphaella turned up at my house in time for dinner.

"You might find my father a little eccentric," I warned her.

Dad got home at the usual time, with the newspaper rolled up under his arm, humming away to himself as he came in the door. I introduced him to Raphaella and they shook hands formally. When he caught my eye, he waggled his eyebrows dramatically, as if to say, "Not bad!"

I stir-fried the vegetables while he sat at the table and read Mom's latest report aloud to us. "I hope your mother isn't getting in too deep," he said, frowning. Then he smiled. "I think they have a few pounds of garlic left at the market if you want me to pick some up for you."

Raphaella laughed. That was his way of saying maybe I had put too much into the stir-fry. But it was too late. I sprinkled some sugar on the veggies, added soy sauce, gave the mixture one last toss, and served it on a plate. I served the fried tofu in a shallow bowl.

Dad tested the veggie dish, pronounced it "groovy" and picked up a chicken wing.

"Maybe you should be a chef instead of a furniture maker," he commented. "What do you think, Raphaella?"

"Agreed."

"I can't boil water without burning it," he said.

I looked at Raphaella. "See what I mean?"

She laughed.

"At least somebody around here likes my jokes," Dad said.

"Dad, do you know anything about that little church out by the trailer park?"

"The African Methodist? A little."

"How did it come to be called African?"

"Because the people who built it in, let's see —"

"Eighteen forty-nine."

His eyebrows shot up and he stopped chewing, then said, "Hmm. How did you come to be interested in the place?"

"I noticed it when I went out to Silverwood the first time. There's a plaque that tells the date."

"The people who built it were descendants of Africans, I suppose. You didn't know about the black settlement in Oro Township?"

"Never heard of it."

"What are they teaching in school nowadays? Never mind, I know the answer to that one. Lots of computers, no history."

"You can say that again," Raphaella put in.

"There was a substantial settlement there in the nineteenth century," Dad went on. "Some say they were runaways from slavery who came through the underground railroad."

"But I've never seen any blacks around Oro."

"Oh, they all left the area long ago. Most returned to the U.S. You should read Elizabeth Maitland's diary. She and her husband were the first to take up land near where the church came to be built. Maybe she mentions it."

"Where can I get it? The library?"

"Don't you remember? It's part of my estate-sale purchase. In fact, you were holding it in your hands not long ago. It's badly damaged, but a lot is still legible. It's a genuine historical record."

I remembered the box of books I had tucked away when the delivery was made, and the musty old volume Dad had showed me that day.

We ate in silence and Dad made a pot of his killer coffee. I brewed tea for Raphaella. While we sipped, a thought came into my mind.

"Dad, you said all the blacks left the area. Why? Too cold up here in the great white north?"

"I doubt it. Most came by way of Ohio and returned there. They have winter there, too. No, it's a mystery. Nobody really knows why they left."

3

After dinner the next day, I met Raphaella at the library. I found her on the second floor, sitting at a large oak table, a small stack of books before her, making notes from a volume that looked like it hadn't seen the light of day for a century or so.

I stood and watched her. Her raven hair hung straight, hiding her face. Why is she so closed in? I wondered for the thousandth time. I knew she liked being with me. Things like that you couldn't fake. And why would she? Nobody was forcing her to hang out with me. I knew she liked the physical side of things, too. Not that there was much. Kissing, hugging, holding hands. She wouldn't go any further, not even when I felt her heart beating against my chest and her breath quick in my ear. She would stop and push me away.

She looked up and saw me. "By the pricking of my thumbs . . ." she said.

"Um, okay."

"Something handsome this way comes."

"I get the feeling you're misquoting someone. Again."

"Shakespeare. The Scottish play. One of the witches."

"Ah," I said knowingly. I didn't have a clue. "Find anything useful?"

"Lots, but it's all background. Let's go to your store where we can talk. I'll fill you in."

At the store we made ourselves comfortable in the office. Raphaella opened up her notes and began.

"Okay, we go back a long way here. Two dates to keep in mind for the time being. After 1793, no one could be enslaved in Upper Canada — or any other British colony, for that matter. People who were already slaves remained so. After 1833, slavery was abolished altogether in Upper and Lower Canada."

"Which really bugged the Americans, I'll bet."

"Keep your eye on the ball here, Garnet. We have a lot of ground to cover."

"Yes, ma'am."

"Speaking of the Americans, relations between them and Britain hadn't improved after the Revolution, in seventeen whatever. You know where Penetanguishene is?"

I put on a stupid face. "Duh, a town up there on Georgian Bay?"

"The British were always afraid that the Americans would control the Great Lakes with their navy, and poor little Penetanguishene sat up there on the water, almost totally isolated, so the Brits got the idea to build a land route there from Barrie. That way, the port could be supplied and defended more easily. Remember, back then this whole area was nothing but wilderness criss-crossed by Indian trails.

"In 1811 a guy named Samuel Wilmot surveyed a road."

"Old Sammy. What a guy."

Raphaella sat straight and rolled her eyes. "No wonder you were in trouble at school all the time. Be quiet and pay attention."

"Did I ever tell you that you're beautiful when you take control?"

"While Wilmot was at it, he surveyed parcels of land on each side of the road for settlers. Why? you might ask."

"I might, but I won't."

"Because settlers could grow food for the

soldiers at the fort and, if necessary, they could defend the road."

"All this is really fascinating, Raphaella, but I don't really see —"

"During the War of 1812–14, the Americans did gain control of the lakes — for part of the war, anyway — so the government of Upper Canada knew it had made a wise decision. They decided to survey the whole area and bring in more settlers.

"The governor of Upper Canada, Sir Peregrine Maitland —"

"Who would name their kid after a falcon?"

"May I continue?"

"Sorry. Proceed."

"Maitland decided to grant some of the land to blacks."

"Hey! Just like Dad said! And Maitland, that's the name of the pioneer who took up land near the church."

"Couldn't have been this Maitland. He lived at York — that's Toronto. Your Maitland must have been a relative. Anyway, here's the rest. Maitland was an abolitionist, and therefore sympathetic to blacks, almost all of them ex-slaves from the U.S. Between 1819 and 1826, twenty-one land grants were made to blacks. Nineteen located their grants, meaning they filed for them, but only eight families actually settled. You had to clear a certain amount of land and build a dwelling before you got ownership.

"Between 1828 and 1831, another forty black families bought land in Oro at a special price. After 1825 the area was opened up to Loyalists and military men, and in 1831 it was opened to what they called indigents — poor people — and a hundred or so white families settled.

"Stop fidgeting — I'm almost done. Between 1831 and 1871, the black population remained steady, but by 1900 they were all gone."

"And nobody knows why they left."

"Exactly."

"How did you find all this out in such a short time?"

"Elementary, my dear Watson. I get books. I read."

She tapped a photocopy of a map. "This shows the survey of the township. The shaded areas are the lots granted to blacks." She picked up her notes and aligned the sheets. I looked at the map.

The Penetanguishene Road, now Highway 93, was clearly marked, and so was Wilberforce

Street to the east of it, named after the Brit whose law emancipated slaves in British territory. It was the first concession settled by blacks.

"Hmm."

"What?" Raphaella asked.

"Look. The lots along the Penetanguishene Road are twice as big as the ones on Wilberforce Street. Old Peregrine was sympathetic toward the ex-slaves but only to a point. Seems he was *against* slavery but not *for* equality. Anyway, now we know why there's an African Methodist church in Oro," I said.

"Right. Although the first generation or two of African slaves apparently hung on to their old beliefs, eventually they adopted the religion of their masters."

"Christianity."

"Yup. Baptist, Methodist and so on. Mostly Protestant. They'd have been Christian for at least a generation before they came here."

"Well," I said, standing and stretching, "all this has been very informative, but it doesn't explain the voices."

"True."

"So, tomorrow we'll go to the township offices and search the title to the land around the church and Silverwood. We need to find out who used to live there." I had a thought. "Hey! Wait a minute. I'll be right back."

I dashed into the workshop and over to the box of books I had temporarily stored in a corner by the door. I picked up Elizabeth Maitland's diary and took it back to the office.

Placing it in the middle of the desk, I explained to Raphaella what it was.

"Great," she said.

The stained and flaky brown leather cover was intact at the front and along the spine, but the back cover had been torn off. The pages were rippled in places, indicating that the diary had gotten wet at some point. It gave off a dry, musty odor.

I opened it at random and flipped a couple of pages. The paper had a yellow tinge and the ink was a sepia color. The handwriting was spidery and difficult to read. On some pages Elizabeth had made line drawings of wild flowers and other plants. Raphaella, to my surprise, recognized all of them.

"She really knew her stuff," she said.

"Maybe this thing will tell us something," I suggested.

"Yeah. It's going to be heavy reading, though."

"I'll start on it tomorrow. Tonight I wait in the bush to see what I can see."

"You mean, *we* wait. I don't want to miss this —"

"Are you sure? The woman doesn't come until midnight. Your mother will kill you."

"I'll deal with my mother later."

chapter 19

We were ready by eleven-thirty, about fifty feet off the trail I had checked out before, the one I was pretty sure the woman was using. It was a mild night, with a touch of breeze. The sky above the treetops was dusted with stars.

Anybody who lives outside the city knows that, at night, the forest is anything but quiet. Added to the faint whisper of the wind in the treetops is the rustle of small animals in the undergrowth, the birdlike chirp of frogs, sometimes an owl's *whoo-whoo* — all of it amplified by the dark and, at least in my case, the imagination.

Raphaella and I didn't speak. We sat down and leaned against a thick maple tree, facing in opposite directions so we covered the trail both ways. I felt foolish — what if she turned out to be a real live woman? — and uneasy at the same time. The bush at night is eerie, and I knew that if I wasn't careful, I'd let the creeps get hold of me. I may have been in techno-mode the day before, but not now.

I jumped when I felt Raphaella's fingers enclose my wrist. Leaves rustled quietly as she got to her knees. I felt her breath in my ear when she spoke.

"She's coming. From your direction."

I peered south along the trail. "I can't see anything, or hear."

"She's approaching. I can sense her."

In the distance, a faint moaning floated out of the dark. Gradually, the sound grew nearer, fuller, rounder, recognizable — the heart-wrenching weeping that was, by now, so familiar to me.

In the darkness, I detected a faint movement. The sharp pressure on my wrist told me Raphaella had seen it, too. I knew in an instant that the woman who slowly came into view was not of this world. I saw her, clearly and distinctly, but at the same time I saw *through* her. She possessed shape and form but no substance.

She was wearing a kerchief, a loose coat open at the front — a man's coat — a long dress under an apron and ankle boots that, like the coat, seemed too big for her. As she walked, a pendant hanging from a cord around her neck bobbed in and out of sight. She was a black woman, with a broad nose and full lips in a face that, if it hadn't been twisted in grief, might have been kindly. She came on steadily downhill toward us, one hand at her chest as if she was holding a bunch of flowers, but her fist was empty. And with her came the cold.

The full weight of her grief fell upon us like a heavy cloak, and her sadness crept into the marrow of my bones, an aching sense of loss so powerful I had the urge to cry with her. Beside me, Raphaella knelt on the dry leaves, her shoulders shaking.

The woman stopped. She stood straight and still, and silent. Slowly, her head turned and she stared at us. I could feel my blood stop in my veins. We're in for it now, I thought.

But, tentatively, she moved off the path. Her footsteps raised no sound as she skirted our position, glancing our way repeatedly, until, once past us, she rejoined the path. The moans rose up again as she continued north through the trees and out of sight.

Without hesitation, Raphaella and I followed her at a distance. I could guess where she was going. We crossed the creek on the fallen log and, after a while, came to the edge of the trees.

The churchyard was brushed with a faint silver light from the moon. I scanned the open area but didn't see the woman. Raphaella tapped my arm and pointed to the right along the broken-down rail fence that bordered the graveyard. The woman was kneeling on all fours, crying harder now, her hands splayed on the ground.

"Jubal," she crooned. "How could you leave me?"

Her voice was strong and rich despite her grief, with an accent I had never heard before.

"I can't take any more," Raphaella whispered, choking back her sobs. "Let's leave her alone."

"Okay."

I led her along the rail fence to the gravel road. The air was noticeably warmer. Somehow, the road was comforting, offering security, normality. I put my arm around Raphaella's shoulders. She was trembling. So was I.

"Come on," I said, and we walked along the road to Silverwood.

2

To my surprise, Raphaella was more upset than I was. As we had walked, the oppressive burden of the woman's mourning had lessened, but in the trailer, at the little dining table, Raphaella was pale and shaken.

I made some tea and we sat at the table, hands cupped around our mugs.

"I wonder who she is," Raphaella said finally. Then, "Were you scared, Garnet?"

"It's strange. I was really scared, until I saw her and when she stopped and stared at us. Then I was more . . ."

"Unbearably sad."

"Yeah."

"I don't know how you've put up with this, night after night."

"It was spooky, but somehow not real. Until now."

"The men weren't there tonight."

"Thank goodness." I took a sip of my tea. "One time when I was in grade ten our class went to the science fair in the city. We were supposed to meet at the bus after lunch in the cafeteria there. It was a nice day so I went outside to sit in the sun and watch the city people go by. There was a bench just near the bus.

"I took off my leather jacket — a birthday present — and closed my eyes. When I opened them I was surrounded by about a dozen guys, a gang. They pressed close to me and I stood up, clutching my jacket. They pushed closer, started swearing, throwing insults, and one of them demanded that I give him the jacket."

"A swarming."

"Yeah, and I'll tell you, it was scary. They pressed me so close I could hardly breathe. Those men from my dream, their voices, remind me of that, and it's worse each time."

Raphaella shook her head. "What have we gotten ourselves into?"

I tried to lighten the mood. "Look at the bright side."

"Which is?"

"I didn't give up my jacket."

3

I got Raphaella back home by 2 A.M. I stopped the van about a block from her place, under an ancient willow, and shut off the motor.

"There's one chance," she said.

"Oh?"

"Yeah. A long shot. Mom knows I was at the library, studying. Sometimes she goes to bed early, nine or so. If she's asleep, I might be able to get in the back door and up to my room without her noticing. It's worth a try."

"Okay. How will I know if you got in all right?"

"If you hear a blast like a nuclear explosion, you'll know she woke up and nabbed me. If not, I'll flick my bedroom light on once. It's the room at the front, second floor."

I watched her run down the quiet street, up her driveway and around to the back of the house. A few minutes later, the upstairs window lit up for a split second, then went dark again.

I started the van and drove back to the trailer.

chapter 20

The first thing we did next day was stop at the African Methodist Church.

"Wait, let me get my notebook," Raphaella said as we got out of the van.

We approached the monument. It was a dull day, muggy and warm, with an overcast sky. The grass was green and damp, and the heavy odor of lilacs hung in the air.

"Read me the names," Raphaella said, clicking her pen. "Hurry. I don't like it here."

Under the inscription "Names of those who worshipped and are buried here," I read out, Banks, Barber, all the way down to Washington.

"Interesting," Raphaella murmured as she jotted the last surname.

"Yup. All Anglo-sounding names except one."

"Duvalier."

At the trailer we sat out on the patio, swatting the occasional mosquito. The green woods were inviting — in daylight.

Raphaella flipped through her notebook. "Here we are," she said. "Some of the names are here. Most of them have 'unknown' noted as the place of birth. Three are from Ohio, one from Guinea, and yes! Duvalier — from Haiti."

"Which explains the French name," I said. "Most slaves lost their African names and were named after their owners. Haiti had a lot of French landowners."

Raphaella's eyebrows arched. "Very impressive," she commented.

"I ain't stupid, you know. I've been doing a little reading myself. Let's finish our drinks and get down to the township offices."

2

We spent all afternoon at the land office, standing in lines, talking with bureaucrats — they were suspicious of us until we explained we were doing a project for school — paying for photocopies, poring over survey maps. Eventually we found out what we wanted to know.

Shortly after the untouched wilderness between Barrie and Penetanguishene was surveyed, Nevil Maitland, a relative of the governor, occupied his land grant on the fourth concession line, just south of present-day Edgar — although the town wasn't there yet and the concession line was just that, a line on a map, not a road. Maitland brought his wife, Elizabeth. They had been living in York.

A few years later, thanks to the governor's interest in helping blacks settle, Jubal and Hannah Duvalier located on the third concession line. Silverwood was on what was once the Duvalier grant. Other blocks of land had been surveyed but not yet claimed. The church was built on land granted by the governor in 1849, which we already knew.

We were also aware, from Raphaella's research, that by the 1830s, grants were made to indigents, families without money or privilege or military service, and even as these European-born settlers were moving in, the blacks were trickling away.

By 1900, the Maitlands had bought up all the land between the third and fourth concessions for more than a mile south of Edgar — including the Duvalier farm — except for the little piece where the church stood. Then their luck seems to have taken a turn for the worse. Piece after piece of land was sold off, including the area where Silverwood stood.

"So the woman we saw is probably Hannah Duvalier," I said as we drove back to Orillia.

"You mean, was."

"Yeah, although I sort of think of her as still, well, not alive exactly, but —"

"I know what you mean. She's probably walking from her cabin to Jubal's grave."

"That's what I was thinking."

"But there's something we still don't know. Why does she walk? Why isn't she at rest?"

"And another thing," I said. "Did you notice where Jubal's grave is? It's outside the church-yard, on the other side of the fence."

"Right."

"Seems strange."

"Yeah. I'll bet there's a story there."

"Something has always nagged at me. How come there are no headstones? Jubal's grave doesn't have one, either."

"Oh, that's elementary, Watson. There are old photos in that little book that has the names listed. The old grave markers were made of wood."

"So they just rotted away over time, like the bodies buried under them."

"Don't be ghoulish."

"You want to know what else I've been wondering all day?"

"Shoot."

"Are the men I hear every night in the bush on that list of names from the monument?"

3

I dropped Raphaella off downtown near her mother's store and picked up a medium pizza, double cheese, pepperoni and mushrooms. Dad was in the showroom, talking with a customer who was eyeing a Boston rocker as if she wanted to eat it. I waved to him and got to work.

Clearing a space on my workbench, I put down the pizza, retrieved a pad and pen from the office, and opened Elizabeth Maitland's diary. Taking care not to drip gobs of pizza sauce onto the valuable object, I turned to the first page and began to read. Before long, the pizza, forgotten, grew cold.

It has long been my purpose to commence a diary, and, having removed to this our new home, I am presented with the perfect opportunity to put into effect this long deferred project.

I record, then, the year, 1825; the place, the Maitland Farm (if, indeed, this place may, without much exaggeration, be so deemed), in the township of Oro, on concession road number four, which is, at present, merely a track; approximately eighty miles north of York. I am compelled by honesty to describe our surroundings as unsettled wilderness, until recently the abode only of savages.

Our rough, log home being recently completed five years after Nevil located his land grant, and our out-buildings, of similar construction (and, it must be owned, appearance) also established; our five acres cleared, we are indeed a homestead. It would be the grossest exaggeration to describe the land as pleasing to the eye, littered as it is with the stumps of laboriously cleared trees, among which the crops are sown, so that the fields resemble a devastated landscape rather than the tidy patchwork of the Old Country; but Nevil has pronounced the soil fertile and the drainage excellent.

I freely admit, dear Diary, that I was held in the grip of not a little fear at the prospect of leaving York and taking up what can only be described as a rough life in the wilderness between Kempenfeldt and Penetanguishene; but Nevil is set on establishing a dynasty in the new world, and has made it abundantly plain that, short of falling upon a cache of gold, the only course of action is to build a life from the ground up, literally. That we are embarked upon an enterprise which may bear fruit only generations hence is a thought constantly on my mind, but I shall not fail to bring to the task all that is in my power.

Elizabeth Maitland didn't say anything in five words if she could use ten, but it was hard to get mad at her. I guess that was the way educated people wrote in those days. Her personality gradually came off the page. She was a brave, hard-working woman who put up with a husband who seemed, at least the way she talked about him, to be narrow-minded, demanding and, more than anything else, ambitious.

The diary might have been interesting to a history prof, or maybe my dad, but not to me. Forcing myself to concentrate, I began to scan the pages more quickly, on the alert for key words. Many pages had been ruined by water that smeared and blurred the ink. Some had fallen out or been ripped out.

Years passed; it was 1827.

Yesterday morning, as I was working in the kitchen garden, there emerged from the trees on the edge of the west field a figure whose uncommon appearance startled me more than I care to admit, for her structure was tall and straight and her skin coal black. She wore homespun, with a bandana of white on her head and stout, if rather the worse for wear, boots on her bare feet.

She greeted me politely, her words conveyed with a lilt and flow not at all familiar to my ears, and said that she and her husband Jubal Duvalier had located on the third line to the west of us.

Her name was Hannah, she said, and

> *she was looking for work, and, as I had*
> *now two babies to care for . . .*

The Maitlands hired Hannah to help in the house one day a week. She was an experienced domestic. She and Jubal had been brought to York by a businessman who had bought them in Haiti years before, moved to the U.S. and ended up in Upper Canada. When their owner died of influenza, they were freed according to his will. Stuck in a foreign country with no money and no means of support, Jubal and Hannah had taken advantage of the land grants open to former slaves and freedmen.

Elizabeth Maitland mentioned Jubal as well as Hannah. Although he was not allowed in the house — Nevil objected "on principle" to having a black man, but not a black woman, under his roof — he sometimes played his harmonica for Elizabeth, who suffered from "the sway of a dark mood" sometimes. I guessed that meant she was depressed.

Another thing Elizabeth hid from Nevil was Hannah's skill in medicine. She gathered plants and made her own "decoctions" and had more than once helped cure the Maitland children's illnesses. She also served as a midwife to some of the black women in the area and, Elizabeth hinted, a few of the whites as well.

I read on. It was 1830.

> *Poor Hannah, so lost since Jubal passed on, and so heart-broken that the African congregation insisted that he could not be buried in the Methodist cemetery, but only on the edge of the hallowed ground. She blames herself, poor woman, though she would not, at first, say why. It was only after no little coaxing on my part that she admitted to me, as a friend, for such we regarded one another, that Jubal was rejected because Hannah practiced what she obliquely called the "old religion."*

I stood up and stretched the kinks out of my back, and was surprised to find it was almost ten o'clock. I put the diary and my notes in an old leather satchel Dad kept in the office and, balancing the box of cold pizza in one hand, turned out the lights and locked the back door.

As I drove to Silverwood, I went over in my mind what I had learned. Raphaella and I had pegged the mystery — or part of it. But what was the "old religion," and why was it so bad —

in the eyes of others — that the congregation had rejected Jubal and Hannah?

Elizabeth was quite a character — educated, intelligent, tolerant when many in her area, like her husband, were not. It must have been tough to leave the civilized life at York and set up house in the bush, bring babies into the world, work from dawn till dusk. I wondered what she looked like. What color was her hair? Her eyes? Was she slender, stout, or tall like Hannah?

Like a rock falling on my head, a thought hit me. I had no idea what Elizabeth looked or sounded like. But I knew what Hannah Duvalier looked and sounded like, because I had seen her ghost.

chapter 21

I almost called Raphaella to tell her what I'd found out, but remembered at the last minute that I couldn't. So I took a shower that did little to wash the musty odor of the diary from my hands, then went to bed. I'd like to say that I felt brave, but I left lights burning in the kitchen and living room, as well as over the door. Surrounded by spirits and voices from the distant past, I felt that I was being set up for some kind of revelation, something I'd rather not know.

But along with fear came curiosity. Hannah and Elizabeth had become real to me. A long time ago they had been close. Why was Hannah haunting the maple bush? Why couldn't she rest?

2

Hannah walked again that night, carrying the weight of her grief like an awful burden to Jubal's grave. On her return, her cries for help seemed, if possible, more panic-stricken than before.

The men swept in just before dawn. When I heard the first muffled exclamation I got up, threw on my clothes and ran outside, hoping to catch sight of them, and hoping not to. I stood shivering in the dark, straining to hear, and then my heart stopped. The voices were moving, not along the path, but toward the trailer. I ran back inside and into the bedroom, sat on the edge of the bed and squeezed my eyes shut.

The hammering of my heart and my own rapid breathing filled my ears. The voices rose in intensity, the words indistinguishable but carried on the same current of horror and anger. The temperature in the trailer suddenly dropped.

Go back!

The exclamation struck me like a hurled rock.

No! No! A different voice.

I hid my face in my hands. The stormy roar

of a small crowd invaded the bedroom, as if the men had surrounded me.

Eighty wish! Like a curse. *Eighty wish!*

The voices clamored and slammed against one another, energized by a violent purpose.

Stones!

Something crashed against the wall.

Get stones!

Another whack. Then another. *Bam! Bam! Bam!* A hail of vicious blows, each one like a hammer blow to my skull. I heard myself moaning.

Bam! Bam!

The pounding went on for what seemed like ten minutes but was probably more like two or three, then abruptly stopped.

Go back!

Fire!

No! The rain!

The arguing continued as the voices receded toward the trees.

I fell back on the bed. After a time, my breathing returned to normal and gradually the rigidity in my muscles eased as the room warmed up. I ached all over — jaws, neck, arms and legs — from the tension. I got up, stumbled to the kitchen, gulped a glass of water at the sink. I had to hold the glass in both hands.

"I can't take another night of this," I said to the empty air.

I threw myself down in a chair, pointed the remote at the TV, waited for the dawn. I barely noticed the figures in an old cowboy movie flickering across the screen. When the grey light of day filled the window I screwed up my courage and went outside.

The rear of the trailer looked as if a crazed mob had attacked it with baseball bats. The aluminum siding was pocked like the surface of the moon, and all over the patio lay stones, none smaller than a double fist.

When I went back inside, I heard music. The movie had ended and some breakfast TV show was on. A gospel group filled the screen, wearing sky-blue choir gowns and belting out a tune.

> *Give me that old time religion,*
> *Give me that old time religion,*
> *Give me that old time religion,*
> *It's good enough for me.*

I laughed at the absurdity. Rocks on the patio. Ghosts in the trees. Television. I put on a pot of coffee, happy to see my hands had almost stopped trembling.

The group sang on. The words spun in my head. Elizabeth Maitland had written in her diary that the congregation wouldn't bury Jubal in the churchyard because Hannah had practiced the "old religion."

I poured a cup of coffee and stood sipping it in the kitchen. On the TV screen, the weather lady had replaced the choir. She stood before a satellite map with moving orange blobs on it.

The old religion. What was that? Raphaella had told me that most American slaves from Africa kept their religion for a generation or two, then gradually converted.

But Hannah had been born in Haiti.

The realization hit me like a train and the cup slipped from my hand, shattering across the floor.

I ran to the phone, jabbed the buttons. "Come on, come on!" I shouted as the ringing sounded.

"Hello."

"Put Raphaella on."

"Who is —?"

"Put Raphaella on the damn phone!"

The words rushed from my throat as soon as I heard her voice.

"It's not *eighty wish!*" I blurted. "It's *Haiti witch!* The men are cursing Hannah for a voodoo witch. They're after *her!*"

chapter 22

I had had enough of Silverwood and its quaint country setting, and I decided that if I spent another night there I'd go crazy. What was I doing, anyway, meddling in events that had happened more than a century and a half ago? What could I do about it? Why me? Was it some kind of sardonic joke that I had been chosen to witness the violent drama played out every night in the bush behind the trailer? What had I done to deserve *that*?

By ten o'clock I had packed up all my stuff and stowed it in the van. Then I set about cleaning the trailer and closing up all the windows. I arranged to have any calls to the trailer transferred to our house, and I wrote up a sign to tape on the door, telling anyone with problems to phone me at home and I'd take care of things from there.

When I had begun to "pull up stakes," as my father would have put it, I had felt a sense of relief, but by the time I drove under the Silverwood sign and turned onto the concession road, relief had given way to guilt. I had made a deal with Dad and I was welching on it. He would lose face with his friend, who had been kind enough to do Dad — and me — a favor, giving me a place to live in return for a job that really wasn't a job. Not once had anyone in the park needed my help. What could I tell him in my defence? That I had been chased away by ghosts? The more I thought about it, the more I felt like a spoiled brat who leaves the party when things aren't going his way. It was a lousy way to convince my parents that I was old enough to decide my own future.

When I got to the crossroads where the Third met the Old Barrie Road, the corner where the church stood, I made a U-turn and returned to the trailer. One of Dad's favorite expressions was, Damned if you do, damned if you don't.

Now I understood what it meant.

2

Raphaella found me on the deck, sitting in the sun and drinking a cup of coffee, when she drove up in her mother's old beat-up compact. She had called ahead and told me she was coming. I was surprised she was driving but had said nothing.

"Boy, the you-know-what really hit the fan, Garnet," she greeted me as she shut the car door.

"I'm sorry, Raphaella. I really lost it this morning. I shouldn't have phoned. Your mom must be in a rage."

She sat down. "No, no. It's not your fault. This was bound to happen sooner or later. Your phone call was just the catalyst. She knew I sneaked in last night."

"Uh-oh."

"Exactly. We fought all morning, a running verbal battle that stormed from room to room. I'm exhausted. In a way it was good, though. A lot of issues came up to the surface. We didn't resolve anything, but now we both know that we've got to work things out, and she won't have her way in everything. I think she must have known this was coming."

"You must feel awful."

"I do and I don't. Mostly I'm relieved. I got the impression she is, too. When you know what you have to face, it makes it easier than guessing."

"How much does she know about us?"

"Only that I'm seeing you. But that alone is enough for her to cope with for now."

"I wish we could tell her the whole thing," I said.

"Be patient." She smiled. "Patience is a virtue, you know."

"Yeah, but the people who say that aren't the ones that have to be patient."

"Anyway, it sounds as if you had the worst night ever."

"Yeah."

"You look pale."

"As if I'd seen a —"

"Don't say it. You think the men are after her?"

It was strange how when we talked about Hannah sometimes we'd slip into the present tense, as if the events were happening here and now. In a way, I guess they were.

"It's the only explanation that makes any sense."

"So we've got to dip into that diary some more."

3

We didn't want to work on the patio within sight of the damage to the back of the trailer, so I carried a chair and a little round table onto the deck and we went to work, occasionally fortified with juice and crackers and cheese. We'd take turns. One would read and, when something relevant came up, relate it out loud while the other took notes.

It was a frustrating search, and boring. The diary contained page after page of domestic narratives, anecdotes about the children as they grew, learned to walk, fell and bruised themselves. A pioneer homestead seemed to be full of opportunities for children to come to grief. And for back-breaking labor — chopping down trees, pulling stumps, hauling stones from the ground to clear more land, building split-rail fences. There were inventories of the output of Elizabeth's kitchen garden, which she seemed very proud of, and lots of musings about Nevil. Elizabeth sometimes betrayed guilt that she didn't love him much.

She also included a little bit of neighborhood gossip, though she often went for a week at a time without seeing anyone outside her family. Here and there was a reference to Hannah.

After Jubal died, Hannah was in a bad way. A pioneer widow with grown children could still run her farm, but one who was childless had three choices: marry again, find work off the land, or leave. Hannah began to work for Elizabeth at least three days a week, often more. She had her own garden, and she made a bit of money ministering to people's illnesses or practising midwifery. She got by, but was very lonely.

Raphaella and I took a break and went for a walk — but not in the bush. Then we set to work again. This time, Raphaella was the reader and I the note-taker.

"Here we go," she announced after a while.

"Find something?"

"Yeah, I think so. This section is badly damaged. There are five illegible pages, then this: '. . . second year in succession. The Spring, having been uncommonly dry and not a whit conducive to sowing; and the rain, when it did finally arrive, falling with such intensity and duration as to ruin the already endangered crop . . .'"

Raphaella flipped over a couple of wrinkled pages with nothing but smears and blurs on them.

"Then this: '. . . as it was last winter. Indeed, trouble comes 'not single spies but in battalions.' Already three children and two adults among the Knox congregation have been carried away by ague, along with at least four among the Methodists, and this added to the poor yields of the last two growing seasons has, for the fist time, caused Nevil to doubt the wisdom of our coming here. There is, among the less educated, much talk of God's wrath and more dangerous speculation about what or whom to blame.'"

That spring, after a tornado had torn through the area and flattened a few cabins and outbuildings and damaged the African Methodist Church, Hannah was not seen again. She failed to come to the Maitland place to take up her duties on the appointed days.

"Listen," Raphaella said. "I think this is 1833. '. . . so worried. Hannah has not been seen, or heard of, for more than a fortnight. I fear that, in her loneliness and desperation, she may have, as have more than a few of the Wilberforce Negroes, abandoned her homestead and gone south; or, worse still, that she may herself have succumbed to the illness that stalks the roads. I shall endeavour to visit her home tomorrow.'"

Elizabeth walked across the west field and through the bush to Hannah's cabin. She described the place in detail. Bunches of herbs and dried flowers hung from the rafters, bottles of "various decoctions" were arranged on shelves. Those were Hannah's medicines. There were no books, as Hannah, like Jubal, had been illiterate. A single chest by the homemade bed held a few articles of clothing. A heavy man's coat hung on a peg by the door. The table and two chairs were neatly arranged under the waxed-paper-covered window, the dirt floor neatly swept.

The place, Elizabeth concluded, was "empty, but not abandoned." Hannah hadn't left. She had disappeared.

More page flipping. Raphaella read a moment, then groaned, "Oh, boy."

"What?" I asked.

Raphaella looked directly into my eyes as tears welled in hers. She began to read once more.

"'She appeared again last night. I heard her pitiful cries carried on the wind from the depths of the forest. Three times this month her soul had, at least so I imagine it, reached out to me. What has happened to the poor wretch? I now fear the worst.'"

Raphaella put the book down and wiped

her eyes. "My god, Garnet. Do you know what this means?"

"Yeah," I said, choking. "Hannah has been haunting this place for more than a hundred and fifty years."

4

Raphaella and I decided to go out for dinner to cheer ourselves up. She drove to town in her mother's car and I took the van. We sat in the Greek restaurant on Memorial Avenue, grimly pushing our souvlaki around on our plates, hardly speaking.

She had wanted to stay with me that night. She knew I wasn't thrilled with the idea of spending another night at the trailer, haunted and scared. But things between her and her mother were bad enough, I argued. Spending the night with the boyfriend would guarantee that she'd be thrown out of the house for good.

"Besides," I explained as Raphaella got into her car in the parking lot, "I'd feel like a coward, running away."

I didn't add that earlier that day I'd almost done exactly that. "And you said that spirits can't hurt me."

"Not physically," she corrected me. "But you don't seem to realize what this is doing to you. You're pale, you're jumpy —"

"But still charming," I joked.

"Leave your cell phone turned on," she said. "All night."

5

I didn't bother undressing. Certain I would not sleep, I lay on the bed and closed my eyes.

The night deepened. The usual domestic noises of Silverwood — parents calling kids in to bed, car doors slamming shut, screen doors slapping, the scrape of chairs on patio stones — faded, and the crickets began their rhythmic song. In the distance, thunder rumbled weakly. My breathing slowed and I felt myself carried to another place.

This is what I saw.

chapter 23

The moon was down when the eight men gathered at the church. In the faint starlight, their faces were planes and pockets of shadow, their whispers a swirl of brief, terse utterances, the words of men urging themselves and each other to action, the casting off of question and doubt. Six of the voices were tinged with the rhythms of the plantation, two with the lilt of Irish field and bog.

They began to move in a knot across the churchyard. Feet thumped on and around Jubal's grave as they vaulted the fence and hurried along the path through the trees — Hannah's path. Determined, driven by frustration and hate spawned by failed crops, empty larders and children burned up by fever, they splashed across the stream, scrambled uphill.

"I can't go through with it," someone hissed. "Let's go back."

"No! No!" came the answer. "We agreed. Keep going."

An argument boiled as booted feet trod the path, drawing nearer to the clearing. All eight came to an abrupt halt when the cabin was in sight. The stink of their own sweat and fear was in their nostrils.

The words were spat out like a curse. "Come on!" and the pack crossed the clearing. The plank door exploded inward under the force of their feet. Three of them rushed inside, then emerged with Hannah struggling and kicking between them, arms pinned behind her, eyes wide with terror. She wore a pendant that bounced on the rough fabric of her nightgown as she struggled, a human face with round holes for eyes.

"Jubal, help me!" she screamed.

There was a split second, a frozen moment, when no one moved, as if her terrified appeal had paralyzed them. Hannah, her nightgown torn at the throat, her chest heaving, gasped for air. The men stood poised, balanced on the edge of determination and indecision.

The sharp stink of urine rose from the

ground at Hannah's feet and broke the spell.

"Haiti witch!" someone cursed. "Child killer!"

"Haiti witch," another hissed.

"Stones! Get some stones!"

Several of the men ran to the wall that bordered Hannah's garden, a wall made from rocks grubbed from the earth and piled in a row. There were so many stones that Jubal and Hannah, like all these men, had built fences with them. Every hand was callused from carrying stones to the edges of fields.

Hannah's two captors dragged her screaming across the yard and flung her to the turf by the low wall. Released, she struggled to her hands and knees, frantic to scrabble away.

The first stone struck her on the back of her head with a sickening *thunk*. Hannah groaned, rolled over, arms extended uselessly to ward off what she knew was coming.

"Help me, Jubal," she pleaded to her dead husband. The second stone slammed into her face, smashing nose and teeth, releasing a gush of blood. The third and fourth hammered her forehead, slashing open her skin, drawing away consciousness. Her blood soaked the earth as stone after stone hailed down upon her.

The eight men, frenzied by the hot odors of

blood and their own terror, snatched up stone after stone. Their arms rose and fell, rose and fell, driving the rocks down onto the unmoving bundle on the ground, breaking bone after bone.

"Enough!" someone yelled finally, and gradually their mania faded. Only the rasp of breath drawn in and out could be heard as the men looked down. At length, someone found a shovel, and Hannah was carried into her cabin and thrown on the packed-earth floor.

It took more than two hours to bury her. During that time a cool, damp breeze swept into the clearing, and thunder rumbled in the distance, creeping nearer and nearer.

When Hannah was in the ground, four men took the excess earth outside and spaded it into her garden as the first of the rain spattered the dry earth. Others stamped the dirt floor flat inside the cabin. Someone rearranged the table and chair by the window. Someone else swept the floor.

"Why you two doin' that? We got to burn the place," another said.

But the storm had hit by then. Claps of thunder shook the small log building and lightning flashed in violent spasms above them. Drained and exhausted, the eight men fled the cabin.

The last man pulled the door shut. "God save us," he muttered, crossing himself, as he followed his companions into the storm.

2

When I woke, a hard rain was hammering the trailer roof and the wind howled, but the thin grey light of morning showed in the windows. I had, I guessed, slept all night, but my body was leaden with fatigue, and my gut churned with nausea.

I got up, stumbled to the bathroom and vomited into the toilet. I shook my head to rid my brain of visions of blood and broken teeth, groans and the sickening thud of stones on flesh. When the retching eased, I stood on wobbly legs under a hot shower, willing the rushing water and steam to wash away the foulness that seemed to crawl on my skin. I wished the shower could wash my memory also.

I towelled off, got into a T-shirt and jeans, put the kettle on for tea to settle my stomach. I fell onto the couch in the living room and stared up at the ceiling. I had witnessed a murder, or rather, an execution, every bit as real as if it had happened on the floor in front of me.

What commandments had she broken that she deserved that death? They had feared her knowledge and power, and stoned what they couldn't understand.

There wasn't a shred of doubt in my mind that what I had seen — whether in a dream or a vision — had happened. Hannah had been killed and buried in her own cabin. The killers had intended to burn down the building so the community would assume she had been consumed by the fire. But the rain had ruined their plan, and they hadn't the courage to return and finish what they had started.

Elizabeth Maitland had discovered that Hannah had not left the area. What a cruel irony that, when she visited Hannah's cabin, she had stood on her friend's grave.

The community would have wondered what had become of Hannah. Did they look for her? Did the men who put her to death walk the woods and fields with the others, pretending to search? Did they carry their guilt with them the way Hannah carried her grief? How many of the locals were secretly relieved that the "Haiti witch" who had brought medicine to their doors or delivered their babies was no longer among them?

3

"My god! They stoned her to death?"

Raphaella and I were sitting on a boulder by the shore of the lake in Tudhope Park. The morning sun had barely cleared the tops of the trees across the green water, and the dew was still on the grass. I had called her as soon as I could, breaking the Rule, and asked her to meet me there.

"What an awful way to die," she said.

I had told her everything I had seen, leaving out no detail. By the time I had finished, she was in tears.

I was close to tears myself. It was as if Hannah had been my friend, as if I had always known her, and the pain of losing her was sharp. I ached for her, the husband snatched from her by sickness, the children she never had, the terror that must have coursed through her like an electric shock when her cabin door had crashed open.

I looked at Raphaella, who sat on the boulder with her legs drawn up, her face in her hands, and I wondered if, before I had met her, I would have felt the empathy for Hannah that gripped me at that moment. Raphaella had opened up parts of me like unused rooms in a mansion, thrown open the doors and pulled the drapes away from the windows.

"You know what I think?" I said finally. "I think the worst thing for her was Jubal's death. She was lost after that. Just like I'd be if I ever lost you."

Raphaella looked straight into my eyes. "You're not going to lose me. Ever."

We got up, took off our shoes and waded into the shallow water. The sand was firm under my feet and the water lapped at my legs. Beside me, Raphaella's light cotton dress was dark where the water soaked it.

I took her hand and led her farther out, until we were thigh deep in the lake, squinting against the brightness and bathed in the warmth of the rising sun. I turned to her and took her into my arms. She put her hand behind my head as she kissed me, the way she had done that day at the opera house.

We kissed again and again, each kiss a promise, while around us the sun danced on the water.

Roy Weeks came home to Silverwood early, putting me out of my job. I didn't care. He apologized for the change in plans and said I was welcome to stay in the trailer as long as I wanted. I thanked him and told him no. Paying for the dented siding on the rear of the trailer took all the money I had been able to save, and Roy gave me a quizzical look when I explained that a couple of drunks must have done it.

I was glad to put the African Methodist Church behind me when I turned onto the Old Barrie Road. I moved into the house on Matchedash — it was hard to think of it as "back home" — taking the front upstairs bedroom with the balcony and the view of Lake Couchiching.

"Watch it up there," Dad had warned with the elfish look on his face that he was never able to hide when he was kidding, "it's an old house. There might be a ghost or two up there."

"Very funny, Dad."

I decided to go to school regularly, get my credits, finish the year properly, and graduate. It would make Mom happy. I missed her and wanted her home where she belonged. I was through with disruption, sick of mystery. I wanted things to be normal again. Predictability and routine suddenly seemed desirable.

A few days later, as I was loading the supper dishes into the dishwasher, the phone rang and shattered my hopes.

2

Dad took the call in the living room, where he had lit a fire, even though it was a warm night. He liked the flames for atmosphere, he said. On the phone, his words were fuzzy and unclear from that distance, but his tone was urgent.

I thought of Mom right away. We hadn't heard from her for a few days. I ran into the living room. Dad stood by his chair, arms hanging loosely at his sides, the phone still in his hand. His face was white, his mouth a firm line.

"What's going on?" I asked.

"That was Wade, at the magazine. Wade Thompson. It's your mom."

"Yeah? *What*, Dad?"

"She's on her way home. She's been . . . She's been hurt."

"Oh, god. What happened? How badly hurt?"

Dad sat down, in a sort of daze. I pried the phone from his hand and set it on the table.

"Dad," I tried again. "What did Wade tell you?"

He swallowed. His eyes focused again. "She — remember she went in-country to do a piece on the refugees? One of the militia bands grabbed her, held her for a day, and left her at the side of a road. Roughed her up, Wade said, but she's all right. Nothing broken. I wrote down the flight number . . . somewhere."

There was a notepad beside him on the table.

"It's here, Dad. She gets in tomorrow."

"Right. Right, tomorrow."

I knew what was going through his mind, the question he wouldn't have asked Wade Thompson. I didn't ask it either.

3

Neither of us slept that night. In the morning we left for the airport far sooner than we had to, only to spend two and a half hours waiting at the terminal, drinking bad coffee from a vending machine. Travelers passed to and fro, walking like zombies, trailing wheeled suitcases behind them.

We didn't talk much. Dad kept jumping up and checking the monitors that listed the flight arrivals, and after the first few times I stopped reminding him that Mom's flight wasn't due for a long while.

At last Qantas 1507 appeared on the monitor, flashing to show the plane had touched down. Dad called out to me and we rushed to the wide double door of gate 5B, but it was another twenty minutes before passengers, tanned and laughing and weighed down with carry-on luggage and souvenirs from Australia, began to trickle through the sliding doors. I almost missed Mom. She was in a wheelchair pushed by a steward, almost invisible behind a wide man with a stuffed koala bear under each arm.

"There she is!" I said.

When he caught sight of her, Dad groaned.

The wrinkled scarf on her head covered most of the cut just below her hairline, but not the ugly yellowy-blue bruise that encircled her left eye, which was swollen almost shut. Her left arm was in a sling. When she got to her feet, aided by the steward, she winced when she took her first step.

When Dad and I approached her, she tried to smile, but couldn't quite pull it off.

"Annie," Dad whispered, "oh, Annie."

She stepped up to him, put her free arm around his neck, rested her forehead on his chest and began to cry. I put my arms around both of them. I hoped that what she felt was what had filled my mind when I left the place where Hannah walked — the overwhelming relief that things are back to normal and you're safe.

"It's okay," Dad whispered, his voice shaking. "We're together again."

Mom didn't say a word on the way home, and we didn't press her. She would have been impatient with falsely happy chatter. She sat with her eyes closed and her head back on the headrest. As soon as we got home, Dad put her to bed and sat in the armchair by her side all day.

When I went to bed, he was still there, reading by the small light beside the bed.

4

Over the next week or so, I watched my mother closely, after I heard her cry out in her sleep that first night. I stayed with her in the mornings until Dad got home at noon, then went to school.

She spent her time reading, dozing, visiting friends, watching a little bit of TV. Sometimes I caught her wandering through the house touching things, as if to convince herself that she was safe now. In the afternoons she and Dad went for a long walk. Gradually her limp faded. On the fourth day she threw away the sling. The bruise on her face began to recede. But the look that came into her eyes sometimes scared me.

She said nothing about her ordeal for a week. Then she let it out — but only to Dad. One evening when Mom had gone up to bed early, he told me.

"She can't talk about it," he began. "She feels humiliated. So don't ask her anything."

"Okay."

"It was like Wade said. A militia band —
they're all over the place, like packs of wolves —
grabbed her and her two colleagues. Teenagers
with guns, out of control, vicious and unpre-
dictable. They let the two men go right away
and took your mother with them. As near as I
can figure out — she wasn't very clear about
this — they wanted to punish her."

"You mean, for what she wrote?"

"No. Scum like them had no idea what she
put in her articles. They were religious extrem-
ists. Fundamentalists who thought females
should stay at home, cover every square inch of
their flesh with black cloth, hide behind veils
and do what they're told. Seeing a woman in
shorts and a T-shirt giving orders to two guys,
driving a jeep — they wanted to make an
example of her."

I was aware of an aching throb at my temples, a wave of unexpressed rage.

"They mocked her, criticized her in broken
English, and when she fought back they slapped
her around, kicked her, beat her up using their
gun butts. When her colleagues found her the
next day she was wandering the road. They
almost missed her. The militia had dressed her
in a black mantle and a veil. On her forehead

they had written a dirty word in red lipstick."

Dad's voice caught in his throat. "She doesn't even wear lipstick," he said. He took a deep breath. "For the first time in my life, I think I could kill somebody. That's what I hate about people like that. They drag you down to their level."

"Dad, did they —?"

"No. But she feels violated. 'Unclean' was the word she used. As if they had raped her dignity. Don't ask her about it," he repeated. "She needs to heal in her own way."

As my father covered his face with his hands I wondered, at another time or in another place, would the militia have stoned my mother to death?

part THREE

I soon fell into a routine that was unusual for me. My teachers had practically died of shock when I began to turn up every day — well, almost every day — for class. I did my best to catch up, plowed through the daily work, clapped together the assignments, survived the tests. I can't say I was any more interested in school than ever, but I kept reminding myself that it would be over in a couple of weeks.

There was one glimmer of enthusiasm supplied by an English essay I had to write, the last one, I hoped, of my life. Paulsen had dreamed up a list of topics — he never let us choose our own; we might actually get interested in something — and when I saw mine, I just about lapsed into a coma on the spot. "Discuss the main conflict in the play *Inherit the Wind*."

"What did you get?" I asked Raphaella in the chaos of the hallway outside Paulsen's room.

"I have to compare any three stories from Matt Cohen's collection *Café Le Dog*."

"Cool title," I offered.

"Yeah. What's yours?"

I showed her. She rolled her eyes and gave me a sympathetic look.

I made the mistake of telling Mom about the assignment. I knew she was getting back to normal when she started badgering me about it.

"When's it due?"

"I don't know. A week or so."

"You don't know the due date? How can you plan it out?"

"Relax, Mom. It'll be fine."

I put off opening the book as long as I could and then, one day when the due date threatened like an unfed dog, I dragged an armchair out onto my little balcony and began to read, making notes as I went along.

Setting: the 1920s, a small town in Tennessee, the buckle on the Bible Belt. A boring opening, people milling around Hillsboro's town square, excited about something, with a few jokes about monkeys. But soon I was hooked. The sinking sun was throwing long shadows across Brant Street when I finished. I went downstairs for dinner.

Back in my room, at my desk, I began to sketch out the conflict. The play was based on a real event, the Scopes trial. Scopes had been an elementary school teacher with progressive views who taught Darwin's theory of evolution, knowing it was against the law. At first, it looked like just another courtroom drama with a slightly interesting twist.

On a simple level the conflict was Scopes against the State of Tennessee. But I was going to argue in my essay that the trial was part of a larger issue: Science vs. Religion, the theory of evolution against the creation story told in the Bible.

I wrote furiously in point form, the ideas almost leaping out of my pen. The big conflict was played out through the personal rivalry of Scopes's lawyer, the civil rights advocate and defender of Darwin's theory, and the prosecutor, a religious fundamentalist opposed to anything that seemed to contradict the Bible.

So, I concluded, feeling very pleased with myself, the main conflict was played out on three levels: Scopes vs. Tennessee; Science vs. Religion; defence lawyer vs. prosecutor.

The next day after dinner I drove out along

the Old Barrie Road. I thought maybe I could clear my head before I converted my notes to essay form. It was a perfect evening, warm and still, and the late-afternoon light illuminated the fields and woods from the side with a warm, brilliant clarity.

I cruised the roads, a plume of dust chasing me along, the rumble of gravel under the tires, the occasional *ping* as a stone popped up and hit the van. I passed a farm. A man and woman came out of a barn, each lugging two pails, as a collie bounded ahead of them across the barnyard. The woman threw her head back as if laughing.

And then I began to think of the men and women and children who had walked the roads and worked the farms long before that couple and I were born. The grass came up every spring, the trees put out new leaves, the wild-flowers in the ditches beside the road returned. There was a permanence to them. But what about all those people? Were they nothing more than boxes of dust in graveyards?

If I'm more than my physical body, I thought, where does the "more than" go when I die? I didn't buy the heaven thing — millions of spirits with or without wings and harps singing hymns and bowing to a god with an inflated ego. But the idea that death was a sort of cancellation, a disappearance, like the flame from a blown-out candle, didn't convince me either. People lived in other people's memory. Was that existence?

As I drove through the hills of Oro I began to feel that the spirits of the dead were, in a way, still there, like the land and the sky. And I realized that I was only beginning to realize what Raphaella had always known.

And then, just as I turned toward Orillia, I slammed on my brakes, pounded the steering wheel and laughed out loud, even though I knew that I would have to start my essay all over again.

2

To say that the main conflict of *Inherit the Wind* was between science and religion, Darwin and Genesis, is misleading, I wrote. That interpretation takes us down the wrong path — trying to decide which viewpoint is right.

Scientists base their belief on provable facts and experiments that can be repeated, on logic and mathematics, on observation and information that we get through our senses. If a statement can't stand this kind of test, it can't be accepted, they say. They are, I thought with a smile, really into techno-mode. On the other hand, the prosecutor, the local minister and the people of Hillsboro accepted faith, revelation, God talking to prophets, and the words in the Bible exactly as they were written. If you have faith, experiment and proof are not necessary.

So, I concluded, the real question of the play isn't Who's right, Darwin or the Bible? It's What is Knowledge? Each side has a different answer to that question and won't accept the alternative.

No wonder the Darwinists and fundamentalists argue, I wrote. They can't get together because they don't agree on what knowledge is.

I got an A+. But I had to share the glory, because, before Raphaella, I could never have written it.

3

It was my mother's wishes and Raphaella that kept my "nose to the grindstone," as Dad happily put it when he realized that I was a half-decent student again. School was a place where Raphaella and I could be together — in the

same building, at least; we shared only one class
— for part of the day, without pressure from
her mother.

Raphaella met my mom, and Mom was very
taken with her. I knew that Raphaella would
tune in on Mom's state of mind and help her.
The two of them seemed to click right from the
start, and before long they were giggling and
talking in whispers like sisters.

"They're making fun of us," Dad would say.

"I know."

"You love her, don't you?" he asked once
when we were alone.

"Yes."

"Good" was all he said.

The *WME* was staged, had its two-week
run, got a rave review in the local paper and a
lukewarm passing mention on Barrie TV. I suffered through the final performance for
Raphaella's sake.

"I hope you realize the sacrifice I'm making," I complained.

"Yes, Garnet. I know you're putting your
entire psyche at risk."

I went to the cast party with her. She didn't
really want to go but felt she should, and decided
definitely to attend once her mother ordered her

not to. It was a pretty wild event, held at the home of the director, a retired teacher from Georgian College who, according to Raphaella, thought he was Steven Spielberg. There was a lot of raucous talk, a lot of booze flowing, and on the patio where the smokers gathered, there was the sweet odor of the glorious weed.

Raphaella and I hung back, like two wallflowers at a grade nine dance. I tried to loosen up with a beer, but Raphaella, who never touched alcohol, was quiet. Around us, conversation swirled like a river, and laughter splashed sporadically across the room. The house was packed, hot, noisy. I felt like a blade of grass, standing elbow to chest in the throng.

When Raphaella went upstairs to the washroom I walked across the damp grass to the shore of the lake. The moon was full, casting sliver lace on the surface of the water. A small sailboat, moored offshore, bobbed peacefully, the halyard *ping-pinging* against the mast.

A sudden raunchy laugh burst my reverie and I went back to the house. The patio was lit up with hanging multi-colored globes, and the two glass-topped tables were littered with beer bottles and empty paper plates. Somebody had ground a cigar butt into the glass.

A young woman stepped clumsily through the sliding door and onto the flagstones. At first I didn't recognize her. In a glittering silver dress with spaghetti straps, a dolphin tattoo on her shoulder, hair artfully arranged to look tousled, she didn't look much like the nun she had played in the *WME*, the one who sings, "How do we solve a problem like Maria?"

"Oh," she said when she noticed me.

I excused myself and reached for the door handle.

"You're Garnet."

"That's right."

On her tanned skin, just above the dress line, was a wisp of cigarette ash, as if someone had used the space between her partially visible breasts as an ashtray. She swayed slightly as she spoke.

"I've seen you around school. I'm a grade below you."

She put a cigarette between glossy lips — her lipstick color matched her dress — and lit it with a plastic throw-away lighter.

"I enjoyed the musical," I lied, unable to think of anything else to say. Garnet the Tongue-tied.

She held her cigarette down at her side,

raised it to take a fast puff, lowered it again in a jerky, awkward motion, as if she was just learning to smoke and didn't particularly like it.

"It was alright." She looked me up and down. I felt like a lamp on sale in a department store. "You're going out with Raphaella."

"That's right."

"She still belong to that cult?"

"That what?"

"I heard she was a member of some cult or other. They're into Satan worship and crap like that. Her mother, too. The one who owns the health food store. Nuts and berries, you know. A watchacallit. A coven. That's why she left Park Street, I heard. People found out and she got hassled." She took a rapid hit off the cigarette. "I'm surprised you didn't hear about it."

"Yeah, well, I guess I don't hang around with the right people."

She didn't get the hint. "I also heard that mark on her face, that stain, sort of, she got in some accident in a ritual," she confided, and sucked on the cigarette. She blew the smoke from her mouth as if it had a bad taste and licked her lips. "Anyway, I'm not saying it's true. I never seen anything funny going on all the time she was working on the show. I just heard things, that's all."

"Excuse me," I said, sliding the door open. "I think my car is on fire."

I entered the house, struck by the racket and heat, seething inside. A shrill female laugh grated on my ears. Somebody jostled me, pushing through the crowd, gripping two beers in each hand by the bottle necks. The background music — some pathetic rock group whose claim to fame was trashing hotel rooms — hurt my ears.

The girl on the patio had made me sick. She passed on hurtful gossip, then disavowed it all by saying she had "just heard it," a kind of verbal hit-and-run. I wanted to find Raphaella and get out of there.

She was by the buffet table, a long linen-covered disaster area that looked as if it had been carpet-bombed. Glasses, some empty, some half full, some knocked over; plates with lumps of uneaten food; stains on the cloth. A wedge of orange clung to the inside of an empty punch bowl.

The director of the *WME* had his arm around Raphaella's shoulder, kneading her upper arm as he spoke earnestly into her ear. In his free hand he held a drink, and he waved it as he talked, slopping liquor onto the carpet.

Raphaella looked my way, caught sight of me, desperately mouthed "Help."

"Excuse me, Mr. Mackie," I shouted above the din.

The director turned my way, a look of irritation on his reddened face. He reeked of whiskey and expensive cologne. He removed his arm from Raphaella's shoulder, raked his fingers through his long salt-and-pepper hair.

"Eh?" he said.

I felt like punching him. Instead, I said, "Miss Skye, your ride is here, waiting in the driveway."

Raphaella smirked and winked. "Why, thank you, Mr. Havelock. You are most kind."

"I can drive you home, dear," Mackie slurred, stepping between us with his back to me. "Be glad to." His voice was syrupy.

"I'd better not," I heard Raphaella say. "It's my boyfriend and he hasn't been the same since he got out of jail. Temper, you see. I just hope," she added, putting down her glass of ginger ale and stepping away from Mackie, "that he didn't bring his biker friends with him this time."

"Eh?" Mackie said again.

He stood with his mouth open as we left him and plowed through the raucous crowd.

We drove to my house and played cards with Mom and Dad. They were trying to teach us to play bridge. After a while, I took Raphaella home.

"We sure are dull," I remarked as I turned onto her street.

"Leaving the party, you mean?"

"Yeah, and spending the evening with my parents. Make sure you mention that to your mother. That I'm boring. Unexciting. Unadventurous. And therefore no threat."

"I already have," she said, laughing, and kissed me good night.

I had decided not to say anything about the girl in the silver dress and what she had told me. Raphaella and her mother, part of a cult? Ridiculous. And yet, I had to admit I had doubts. The key to a cult was, I supposed, secrecy. Raphaella had things that she wouldn't talk about. And she had studied the occult. She knew about numerology.

I drove home. Whether I was angrier at Silver-dress for the gossip or myself for my doubts, I couldn't tell.

chapter 26

There was a story I read in elementary school one day when my grade eight teacher became so exasperated with my behavior that she sent me out of the room.

"Just go," she snapped. "I don't care where. Just go."

I wandered up and down the halls for a while and ended up in the library, and the librarian put me in a corner with an old volume of Greek myths.

There was a musician named Orpheus whose skill on the lyre was so heavenly that even birds and animals fell under its spell. Humans couldn't resist its charm. Orpheus's wife was named Eurydice, and he loved her with all his soul.

Ordinarily a tale that began that way would

have turned me off immediately, but this time the force of the story pulled me along.

Orpheus and Eurydice were happy together. Along came the villain, the son of a god, whose name I forgot, but it began with an *A*. He was hot for the lovely Eurydice, and being half-god, he was used to getting what he wanted. One day, when Orpheus was off on a gig somewhere, A. visited Eurydice, and, when she told him to get lost, he attacked her, cursing her and tearing at her clothing. Running frantically away from him, she stepped on a poisonous snake and it bit her. She passed away soon after.

Orpheus was numb with grief, and his music died with Eurydice. He saw no reason to continue to play, or to live either. So desperate was he that he decided to go to the underworld, Hades, to find Eurydice and stay there with her. He took his lyre with him.

Orpheus had to convince the Queen of Hades, Persephone, to let him find his wife and remain there with her. Orpheus, she said, could take his wife home from the underworld. But there was a condition. "Eurydice will walk behind you on your return to the mortal world," she told Orpheus. "This you must believe. You must prove your love for her. Do not look back. If you do, our bargain is forfeit."

Orpheus began his homeward trek, but with each step his worry and his doubt increased, until, finally, he gave in to his insecurity and turned around. Briefly, he glimpsed his beloved wife. She raised her hand to reach for him, then dissolved into thin air.

And one day near the end of June, during the final exam period, I let my curiosity about Raphaella and her mother, and my frustration that Raphaella still closed a lot of her life from me, overwhelm me. I broke faith with her by going against my promise to wait and let her explain things in her own way, in her own time.

I went to confront her mother.

2

The Demeter Natural Food and Medicinal Herbs store — a name so long it barely fit on the sign above the window — was on the west side of Peter Street across from the art gallery in the Sam Steele Building. One afternoon, when Raphaella was at the school writing her geography final, I took a deep breath, pushed open the door and stepped in.

It was a small store, suffused with the strong, clean odor of dried herbs. I saw Mrs. Skye immediately, behind a counter, her back to the door. She tossed a look over her shoulder, smiled automatically, obviously not recognizing me — no surprise, since she'd only seen me through the van's windshield.

"Be with you in a minute," she said, turning away. "Can't stop in the middle of this prescription."

She stood before what can only be described as a wall of small drawers that rose from a table with a set of scales on it, along with three or four wooden mortar and pestle sets of different sizes, a stack of small paper bags and a few bottles of liquid. Each of the drawers was no bigger than an envelope and had a small wooden knob on it.

She worked quickly, consulting a piece of paper, pulling open a drawer, extracting material that looked like leaves, sticks or dried flowers, shutting the drawer, weighing, adding the results to one of the brown bags, going to another drawer.

She was slender, like Raphaella, with short brown hair cut without style. She was wearing a green smock over a red T-shirt, and jeans. Not exactly a fashion statement. Not exactly a cult member either.

I took the chance to look around. There was a machine to make peanut butter at the end of a counter beside a canvas sack of peanuts. On the walls were shelves of bottles and jars, packages and boxes of various health foods and supplements. There was a bookcase, too. I scanned some of the titles: proper diet for health, proper diet for cancer and heart disease sufferers; acupuncture and acupressure. There were a few books on midwifery and a number on "natural religion." A room at the back was devoted to dry goods — more kinds of beans and peas and rice than I knew existed; cereals; spices and herbs, all organically grown.

I made my way back to the counter. Whoever had made it knew what he was doing. The front was tongue-and-groove pine, the top six-inch pine planks, all finished in a natural color. On the top were pamphlets on Orillia's Mariposa Bike Trail, membership forms for Amnesty International and Greenpeace, and one booklet that said, "Your local golf course: an ecological disaster." I know where Raphaella gets her T-shirt captions, I thought.

Raphaella's mother was now sitting at a small

desk, writing something. I cleared my throat, anxious to get things over with. She looked up, stapled the piece of paper she'd been writing on onto the bag, then stared at me as if searching her memory for my mug shot. She wore an ankh on a gold chain around her neck, like Raphaella's.

Just as her eyes widened in recognition, I spoke. "Mrs. Skye, I'm Garnet Havelock."

She stood up.

"Raphaella's boyfriend," I added.

"It's Ms., not Mrs. I recognize your voice. From the phone. Only you don't sound so rude today."

Well, this is getting off to a great start, I thought. I decided to ignore her barb. "I wanted to come and introduce myself." I held out my hand to shake with her.

She didn't move. "I see," she said. Her voice was quiet and firm, like Raphaella's. Confident.

"I was hoping we — you and I — could, well, get to know each other. Break the ice, if you see what I mean."

She didn't move, didn't speak, just looked at me as if I had a target on my forehead. A tiny, sharp edge of anger sliced into me. She was making no effort to be friendly. She wanted me to feel uncomfortable, foolish.

"Raphaella doesn't know I'm here. She had nothing to do with this."

Still no response.

"So, are you going to talk to me or stare at me for the rest of the day?"

She put the paper bag down on the desk and crossed her arms over her chest.

"I'm in love with your daughter," I said, trying to be as self-assured as she seemed to be, and failing. "She loves me, too. I think that's what she'd say. If you asked her, I mean."

"I have."

"And?"

She nodded. Once. We stood looking at one another for a moment. I realized I was wasting my time.

"Well, I just wanted to introduce myself," I said. "Goodbye. Sorry to bother you."

I turned to leave, had my hand on the doorknob, but spun around instead of opening the door. She hadn't moved.

"What is it with you, anyway?" I almost shouted. "What's wrong with me that I'm not good enough for her?"

Ms. Skye shook her head. "That's not it. You wouldn't understand."

"That's incredibly condescending," I

snapped. "And bigoted if you ask me —"

"I didn't ask you," she cut in, her tone as calm as before. Nothing makes me angrier than when I'm mad and someone talks to me as if she's describing how to wash a pot.

"This isn't about you personally," she added.

"Look, Ms. Skye, if *this* isn't personal, *nothing* is."

"It isn't anything to do with you," she repeated, adding dismissively, "Now, if there's nothing more I can do for you . . ."

"I'm sorry I wasted your time," I muttered, dying to say more. I turned away and quietly closed the door behind me.

chapter 27

If I expected Raphaella to fall into a rage when she found out I'd gone to see her mother — somehow I knew Ms. Skye wouldn't pass up a chance to make me look bad — I had misjudged her there, too. Icy calm was her response. I phoned repeatedly, and each time her mother would say in a flat, almost bored tone, "She doesn't want to talk to you."

"How do you know she doesn't?"

And she would hang up.

I drove over to the house half a dozen times, rang the doorbell, whacked the knocker. No answer. I went to the store, and Ms. Skye said triumphantly, "You come back and I'll slap a restraining order on you."

A few days later a note came in the mail.

"Please don't contact me again," and it was signed, "R. Skye."

A week passed. I sank into a swamp of guilt and despair. One minute I'd be seized by anger. What, after all, had been my big crime? The next moment I hated myself for what I had done, not just the stupidity, but my betrayal. Raphaella had trusted me, had placed faith in my promise, and I had sneaked around behind her back like a tenth-rate private detective, all because some half-drunk airhead had passed on a bit of malicious gossip.

I wrote a letter to Raphaella, trying to explain myself, asking her to forgive me, but it came back unopened. I stood across the street from the Demeter store, ignoring Ms. Skye's threat, hoping to see Raphaella. No luck.

Another week passed.

My parents steered clear of me after the first time Mom innocently asked, "Where's Raphaella these days?" and I almost bit her head off. Every day I'd go to the shop and work on the Maitland restorations, trying to lose myself in my work, often staying past closing time. But a lot of the time I'd think about that first day when Raphaella had sat in the chair and I had worked on the slat for the baby crib while we talked.

When I got home, unless it was raining, I'd go for a long run along the lakefront, avoiding Tudhope Park. I sought to tire myself, hoping I could fall asleep easily. I tried to pass my free time reading, but I couldn't concentrate. Food didn't interest me. Nothing did.

Another week passed.

I knew then that I had lost her. For good.

As I worked in the shop, I wondered if I could ever get used to living without her, if I could fill the empty space inside me. And that was when I started to think about Hannah, her grief at losing Jubal. And I began to talk to Hannah inside my head. I lost someone, too, I'd say, but it was my own fault. I wish I could figure out a way to get her back.

Then it dawned on me that there was something I could do for Hannah. It wasn't a completely selfless thought. If I could help her, maybe I wouldn't feel so worthless.

2

"Dad, we've got some seasoned oak planks out back. Do you mind if I use some for a personal project?"

My father looked up from the ledger that lay

open on the office desk. He searched my face. He and Mom had been treating me like an invalid lately, wondering what was going on and only halfway to an answer when Raphaella had dropped out of the picture.

"Hey, you don't have to ask. You know that. Back there," he pointed at the shop door, "you're in charge. What's the project?"

"Oh, nothing really."

"Sounds interesting," he said.

3

My first step was a visit to Ontario Provincial Police headquarters on Memorial Avenue, a huge complex that looked like a cross between an airplane hangar and a factory. I talked with the director of the forensic division. I told him I needed some information for a school project and he was very helpful. It was only after I'd left that I remembered school had been out for a couple of weeks.

Next, I selected two one-by-six boards, lined them up on the pipe clamps so their grains ran opposite to one another, glued the edges and tightened the clamps. When the glue dried, I'd have a twelve-inch plank. I left the wood for a couple of days before removing the clamps and cutting a number of lengths from the plank. I took four pieces and glued and clamped two sets of two for the top and bottom of the box I was making. The pieces that would form the sides I routed along both sides, then cut the dovetails into the ends. They would ensure strong and lasting corners. More gluing and clamping, along with careful use of the square, produced a bottomless and topless box.

The next day I spread glue on the touching surfaces, fitted the bottom and fixed it in place with brass screws. I drilled and countersunk holes in the top, which would not be permanently attached until later, then prepared the wood for the finish, sanding it within an inch of its life, making it as smooth as glass.

I selected a natural oak stain-sealer and applied it by hand with a rag, rubbing it in, making sure the color was even. I set it aside to dry.

Over the next week I applied a coat of plastic finish each morning after lightly sanding the previous day's job, until I had a deep matte finish on the box, so clear I could see my face in it.

I was testing the top for fit one last time when I heard Dad calling from the showroom.

"Garnet! Someone here to see you."

"Send 'em back," I answered.

I sank my fingers into a tin of hand cleaner and began to work the cream into my hands, dissolving dirt and stain. The stuff had an awful smell, but it did the job. A few paper towels removed the cream from my hands. I went to the sink to wash with soap and water. My back was to the door. When I looked up, Raphaella was standing there.

She was wearing a canary-yellow T-shirt, white shorts and leather thong sandals. Her hair was loosely held at the back of her neck. Against her tanned skin her birthmark seemed faded, subdued.

My heart practically leapt from my chest. I made myself remain calm. Maybe she was here for something that had nothing to do with her and me, I cautioned myself. Maybe she was working on another show and wanted to borrow more antiques or something. I stood there in my stained apron, wiping my hands on a ratty face towel, afraid to speak.

She came to me and put her arms around my neck. My eyes stung. I hugged her tightly, as if I were drowning.

"I missed you," I whispered, almost crying.

"I broke my promise. I'm sorry."

"I missed you, too," she answered. I felt her tears on my neck. "I was mad at you, hurt. But I broke my promise, too. Remember that day in the park? I said you wouldn't lose me."

I didn't deserve her forgiveness, but I said nothing.

"I expected too much of you," she whispered. We stood like that for a while, until Dad came to the door.

"Oopsy-daisy," he said, spinning on his heel and disappearing.

Raphaella dropped her arms, wiped her eyes with the backs of her hands. "'Oopsy-daisy'?" she said.

"Yesterday he called me Daddy-o."

She laughed.

We stood there like two losers on a blind date. Then Raphaella's eyes fell on the oak box.

"That's a beautiful finish," she said. "What's the box for?"

"Well, you're going to think I'm crazy," I replied. I told her what I had in mind.

"I want to help," she said.

"We're going to need money and a lot of equipment."

"Okay."

"I love you," I said.

"I know you do. I never doubted it."

"Uh-huh. And?"

"And what?"

"This is the part where you say, 'I love you, too.' You forgot."

"Oopsy-daisy," she said.

chapter 28

I had planned it carefully — and secretly.

One thing was on our side: we had all the time we needed. We assembled a collection of gear that almost filled the van. A large tent, plastic tarpaulins, leather gloves, pails, flash-lights, lanterns, garden trowels, paint brushes, a couple of metal flour sifters. What I couldn't scrounge, I bought.

I wanted to move the equipment in at night because the plan was illegal. Once we were set up we'd be out of sight and we'd be able to work in daylight. I parked the van off the side of the road by the stone monument. I helped Raphaella struggle into her backpack harness and shouldered my own pack. Moonlight bathed the graveyard, but when we entered the maple forest we had to use our flashlights.

It took us three trips to get all the gear to the clearing. By then it was close to midnight. We left quickly, having no desire to meet Hannah on her nightly walk.

The next day we prepared the site, growing accustomed to the chill as we worked. We cut and raked away the grass and weeds that grew inside the ruins of the cabin. Afterwards, we pitched a family-sized tent over the area. Once we had cut away the nylon floor of the tent, we had a weatherproof area. Setting to work with spades, we skimmed off the turf from the ground, the matted roots fighting us every step of the way, and hauled the chunks of sod outside. After a full afternoon of panting and sweating, we had cleared the floor of the tent — once the floor of Hannah's cabin — down to black earth.

"Do you think we'll have to go very deep?" Raphaella asked, wiping her dirt-smudged brow with a hanky. Black soil was caked under her fingernails and ground into the skin of her hands.

"I doubt it."

"Should we make a grid with string, the way the arch- eologists do?"

"No," I said, looking around, "not necessary."

"That was a joke, Garnet. Lighten up."

Tired and sore, we called it a day.

2

The next morning, we were back, just after sun-up, well supplied with coffee, juice, sandwiches and chocolate bars.

"We don't want to be in the middle of things when night falls," I said.

Once inside the tent, with the little portable radio playing, we began. I scratched a line down the center of the dirt floor, and we each worked away from the line to the opposite wall.

Digging with a garden trowel was tedious and exacting. We put the dirt into plastic buckets and emptied them outside the tent. We took a break for lunch, sitting outside in the clear air, glad to see sunlight after hours bent over inside the gloom of the tent, but wearing sweaters because, despite the weather reports on the radio that reminded us it was 28 degrees Celsius that day, the clearing was chilly.

We watched, fascinated, as squirrels and birds would approach the clearing and then, as if they'd hit an invisible force field, veer away. As we ate and talked, clouds moved in from the southwest, and by the time we got back to work, the sun was obscured. Occasionally, the radio crackled. There must have been lightning somewhere.

As the afternoon wore on, the cool air became more humid in the dimly lit tent. We painstakingly dug and scraped, filling buckets, emptying them, filling them once more, over and over, until we fell into a kind of trance.

I was outside, dumping a pail of dirt beside the pile of sod we'd made the day before, stretching the kinks out of my aching back, looking up at a sky that promised rain, when the music coming from the radio inside the tent suddenly stopped.

"Garnet, you'd better come in here," I heard.

Raphaella was on her knees in the two-foot depression we had dug, brushing at something with a small paintbrush.

"Hold the light closer," she said. "I think I've found something."

My eyes locked on the curved, brownish-grey shape that winked in and out of sight as Raphaella plied the brush. Carefully scraping away dirt with a kitchen knife, then whisking it aside, scraping again and brushing, she slowly uncovered the round outline of a cranium.

"How can we be sure it's Hannah?" Raphaella asked.

"It must be."

I realized we were whispering.

"Wait." Raphaella used the knife again, this time beside the skull, and prised from the dirt a black cameo.

"That's it," I blurted. "I saw it in my dream. That's all the proof we need."

3

Both of us were energized by the discovery. Not being an archeologist, I wasn't sure what the best procedure would be. We had to make sure we got everything; we couldn't leave a foot bone or a finger end behind. The job had to be complete.

"I think we should uncover all of her, leaving each bone in place, before we move anything. What do you think?" I asked Raphaella.

"That seems best. If we take out one bone at a time we might overlook something."

"And," I reminded her, "we have to be done before midnight."

I could see her throat work when she gulped. She shuddered.

"Right. Why don't you get started, and I'll

go back to the van. We're out of juice, and I'm thirsty."

"Good idea."

It was a muggy evening, humid and still, and a few mosquitoes hummed their irritating little one-note tune inside the tent. I lit a mosquito coil in one corner and went back to work.

I began to dig with the trowel, feeling like an expert now as I quickly but carefully removed dirt from around the skull, then worked my way down the vertebrae. I had uncovered a shoulder and upper arm when I heard footsteps rapidly nearing the tent. The flaps were swept aside and Raphaella stooped to get inside. She was panting.

"What's wrong?" I asked her.

She fell to her knees and dropped a plastic supermarket bag beside the dug-out area. I heard cans knock together.

"I think those men are in the woods somewhere." She picked up her trowel and began to scrape in the dirt.

"Where did you see them?"

"I didn't. I sensed them."

"Uh-oh." A cold blade slid though my ribs.

We pressed on. The excavation wasn't difficult, because the earth was loamy, but it took time. We could have dug up the area with shovels and sifted the earth, like miners, but that seemed disrespectful.

"Do you feel it, too?" Raphaella said after a while.

"Yeah. They're out there, all right. But we're almost done."

When we had uncovered the entire skeleton, we sat in the dirt for a moment and looked at Hannah's remains. Her killers had buried her in the fetal position. Her legs were crossed at the ankles, her head rested on one hand. She looked almost peaceful.

But every major bone in her body — arms, legs, skull, four ribs, her pelvis — was broken.

"My god," Raphaella moaned, "look what they did to her."

Reverently, careful to leave nothing behind, we placed Hannah's remains in the oaken box I had made, kneeling beside her in the dirt as we worked. I cleaned the pendant, rubbing it with a rag until it glowed. It was made of some charcoal-colored stone, not wood as I had first thought.

"I think Hannah would have liked you," I said. "I'll bet she'd want you to have this."

"We've got a lot in common, I guess," she replied, "but the pendant should stay with her."

"Okay, if that's —"

The voices interrupted me, that same angry background rumble, all talking at the same time, as if in dispute.

Raphaella moaned. "They're here."

I laid the pendant in the box and put on the

lid, using brass screws to secure it, fumbling with trembling hands.

"Done," I squeaked nervously. "Let's get out of here."

"I don't think they can hurt us physically," Raphaella assured me, but she didn't sound very confident.

I recalled the pockmarks on the back of the trailer, but said nothing.

When we emerged from the tent, it was twilight, and the smell of rain was in the air. The eight men were lined up along the fencerow, glaring in our direction, as if waiting for us. I saw them and saw through them. They were shades, but they were as frightening as any mob of real men, rough and strong looking in homespun shirts and worn overalls and heavy boots. They stood, silent now, and stared, not at me or the box that I held in my two hands, but at Raphaella.

"Stones," someone whispered.

The wave of terror that struck me was almost physical. One of the men slowly lifted a stone from the wall.

"Get stones," he said. One after another, the men obeyed.

"Raphaella, run!"

Raphaella sprinted toward the path and I turned to follow. A stone struck my elbow, knocking the box from my grip. I stooped to pick it up, hunching my shoulders, when another rock slammed into my back. I dashed into the trees, more stones thumping to the ground behind me.

It was awkward, running with a pack on my back and my hands full, and I knew I was moving too slowly to stay ahead of them for long. I pushed on, stumbling, my breath like fire in my chest. Where the land began to slope, the men caught up to me. The acrid stink of their sweat and the damp cold that seeped from them enveloped me. Oh, god, I thought, awaiting the crash of a rock on my skull. But they thundered past me, like a river flowing around a boulder. Panting and cursing, they left me in their wake, closing on Raphaella. She ran on, hair flowing behind her.

"They're gaining on you!" I shouted. "Drop your pack!"

I tripped on a root and slammed into a tree at the side of the path. I fell to my knees, paralyzed and gasping.

Without slowing down, Raphaella shrugged off her pack and let it slide from her shoulders.

But as it fell it caught her heel. She pitched headlong to the ground and cried out, arms and legs flying as she rolled like a tossed doll down the slope and, with a splash, came to rest in the creek.

In an instant her pursuers were upon her. They encircled her to prevent escape, and each one, holding a stone in his two hands, raised it above his head. Unable to breathe or rise to my feet, I watched helplessly. It was as if, in that instant, we had all fallen back through time. A woman surrounded by violent men about to stone her to death and obliterate what they feared — her knowledge, her strength, her independence and a nameless quality, a something that they could never know or possess.

"No!" I shouted uselessly. "No, don't!"

Raphaella did not cringe. She struggled onto all fours, then rose to her knees. Her shirt was torn, her hair a tangle of small sticks and leaves, her forehead scraped.

"Witch!"

In one quick motion, she took her ankh in one hand, pulled it over her head, dipped it into the creek and held it up. "By the power of water, I command you," she said through clenched teeth.

A few of the men looked at one another and shuffled their feet, as if gathering strength.

"By the power of water, I command you!" Raphaella repeated, her voice stronger.

She bent and clutched a handful of damp dirt and held it out. "By the power of earth, I command you!"

As one, the men stepped back, lowering their arms.

Able to draw breath by then, I freed myself from the backpack and ran to Raphaella, breaking into the circle of men. They fell back in an uneven line at the edge of the stream. The stench was overpowering.

Raphaella rose slowly to her feet and, still holding her ankh in one hand, stepping carefully backward, pushed me across the creek. Her face was a mask of determination.

"Do you still have your matches?" she whispered, panting.

I dug the book of paper matches from my pocket.

"Get ready," she said. Then, to the men, "By the power of air, I command you!"

I caught on. Opening the paper cover, I twisted a match from the book and pressed the head against the strike strip.

"By the power of fire, I command you! Go!"

My hand jerked. The tiny match burst into flame, sending off a sulphurous little cloud of black smoke. Dropping their stones, the men ran, dispersing like blown mist into the trees.

chapter 30

Breath rasping in and out with the aftershock of fear, I began to brush away the bits of wood and leaves from Raphaella's hair, willing myself not to think about what I had just witnessed. I pried the ankh from her grip and hung it around her neck.

"Are you all right?" I asked.

She straightened her soaking-wet clothing and touched the now bleeding scrape on her forehead. "I think so. What about you?"

"I'll have a few bruises tomorrow. I thought we were in for it."

"Me, too."

"Wait here."

To give myself time to think, I crossed the creek and walked back up the path, retrieving the box and our two backpacks. I helped

Raphaella into her pack, handed her the box, and slipped into mine.

"That was incredible," I said, shaking my head. "How did you know what to do?"

"I didn't. I was in the creek, soaking wet, and the idea just slipped into my mind. The four elements, water, earth, air and fire.

"You had them completely under your control."

"Not really. The important thing is that *they* believed I had some sort of power."

"Well," I said, looking around the darkening forest, "it seemed to work."

"I don't think I've ever been so terrified."

I took her hand, which was trembling almost as much as mine. "Let's go," I said.

2

By the time we got to the rail fence on the edge of the churchyard, a light rain had begun to fall. We retrieved our raincoats and a shovel from the van.

Nothing marked Jubal's grave, but I had seen Hannah kneeling there, so I knew exactly where it was. The sod was as tough as leather, but beneath it the earth was easy to dig. I went down about three feet, placed the box in the hole, and looked at Raphaella.

"No. There's nothing we can say," she assured me.

I buried the box and replaced the sod, stamping it into place firmly. The air warmed up noticeably. The grave was almost invisible. In a week, no one would be able to tell that someone had been digging there.

"Well," I said, "they're together again."

Dirty and wet and sore, we headed toward the van. As we crossed the grassy churchyard, Raphaella put her arm around my shoulders.

"You know what?"

"What?" I asked.

"You are a good man, Garnet Havelock."

chapter 31

With school behind us, Raphaella and I were suddenly confronted with our futures. I had settled on what I wanted to do long before, and my plans to apprentice to Norbert Armstrong in Hillsdale were still firm. I was looking forward to it.

But with Raphaella, it was a different story. She was at loose ends. She had no plans for university or college because, with all the pressure from her mother, she hadn't applied. She liked working in the theatre, but it wasn't really a career option, especially as far as her mother was concerned. She could keep at it as a volunteer in community shows. She didn't mind working in the Demeter, she said; she even liked it.

"But I can't see myself growing old there, either," she told me the day after we buried

Hannah. "Oh, it's a mess. I can't separate what I really want from the temptation to spite Mother."

We had taken the aluminum fishing boat that Dad kept at a family friend's boathouse and putted out to Horseshoe Island, lowered the anchor, and gone swimming. Afterwards we lay side by side on the bottom of the boat, looking up into a painfully blue sky, and talked as the lake gently rocked us.

"As long as we're together, I don't care what I do," Raphaella mused.

"But someone as smart and talented as you," I began, and stopped. I sat up and looked down into her eyes. "Look, I'm not saying there's anything wrong with working in a store, especially if it's yours, and you're interested in it. I'm doing that now, and so is my father. And," I added carefully, "I'm not trying to butt in where I don't belong. All I'm saying is, I'd hate to see you trapped into something you'll end up hating. I think you're right to take your time and think things over."

Raphaella closed her eyes. "Trapped is the word, all right. I feel like I've been trapped all my life. It's as if . . ." She opened her eyes. "Well, suppose there's this room, and you really like it, you like being in it. But somebody says to you, 'You *must* live in this room. There's no choice. And you can never live anywhere else.' Even if you like the room, you'd feel resentful. See what I mean?"

I didn't, not exactly, but I nodded anyway.

"You'd always wonder, Why can't I go into other rooms? What are they like? Maybe they're better than this. Maybe this room only *seems* nice because I've never had the chance to try other ones. I sound demented, don't I?"

"No, I understand what you're saying," I replied, catching on. "What bugs you is not having the choice. It's wondering, if you could choose, what would you really want?"

"Exactly. No wonder I love you. You're smart, too. And you look pretty good in that bathing suit."

"You want to change the subject," I said.

"Yeah. There's something you should know."

As if she had opened a door in herself that had been closed for so long the hinges creaked and the wood groaned, she told me.

2

"I've been afraid to tell you these things for a lot of reasons," Raphaella began. "At first, I didn't want you to laugh at me. I've had enough of that in my life to last a century. Later, I was afraid you'd dump me. No, don't say it. You think you wouldn't have, but don't be so sure. I'm not blaming you; I'm just saying. Now I'm confident about us. Especially after that night in the woods.

"I want to tell this right. You know I'm not . . . that I'm unusual. My grandmother — on Mother's side — was also, well, I guess the modern word is psychic. She could feel things, as if she were a string on a musical instrument that vibrated is sympathy with her surroundings. I was very young — I can't remember how young — when it first happened to me. I recall being terrified. But Gram taught me not to fear the gift, and finally to appreciate and treasure it.

"Mother says that, in our family, the gift skips a generation. She doesn't have it, but I have. I can't give up my gift or ignore it. I know that. And I don't want to. Denying it would destroy me. It's part of what I am, more than the shape of my nose or my shoe size or this mark on my face. But I'm certain now that I don't have to give it up. Being with you doesn't mean I have to deny what's part of me. And I know you wouldn't expect me to. That's what I've told Mother, what I tried to make her understand. You don't take away from me; you add to me.

"But being different isn't the only thing I've hidden all my life.

"You asked me once about my father and I ignored your question. I know, it's not the only question I've dodged or ignored, so don't give me that look. The truth is that, other than in the biological sense of the word, I don't have a father.

"I come from Edmonton originally, but I don't remember it because Mother and I left there when I was five. And I don't recollect much about my father.

"He was a lawyer in a big firm, and he was away from home a lot of the time. He'd come home late. I'd already be in bed and he'd come into my room and kiss me good night. Then one night he didn't come home at all. Suddenly, it was horrible around our house, with a dark atmosphere of doom and secrecy and disgrace, my mother crying all the time and Gram trying to comfort her. I didn't know what was going on, why things had changed so fast.

"Slowly, I gathered that I was losing my father because he had done something bad, he had made our lives dirty, but I was too young to take it all in. It was as if fate had come by one day and turned out all the lights.

"It happened at a Christmas party at his firm. He came on to a woman who worked there. She claimed he wouldn't take no for an answer. He forced her. It sounds so cliché when I talk about it, something you'd see in a second-rate TV movie. A couple of people at an office Christmas party who had too much to drink.

"My father claimed she was willing. He was found guilty anyway. The thing was, my mother told me later, when I was old enough to understand better, she would have supported him, believed him, but, during the trial, a lot of stuff came out. Stuff about his life. He had a couple of girlfriends on the side. He'd been unfaithful for years.

"That's what destroyed my mother. The humiliation. Finding out in a public courtroom, in front of people. Like I said, she could have held up under the trial, stood behind him, but when the other stuff came out, she broke.

"So we moved away, and my father is never, ever mentioned. I don't miss him. All that was a long time ago. I'm glad I have no feeling for him, because if I did it would probably be hate, and I don't want to feel like that about anybody. I've seen what it does to my mother.

"I don't know how you get over something like that, the betrayal and the debasement. It made my mother bitter, and it turned her against men. She has no use for males. That's why she gets so unreasonable with me. She's kept me away from boys all my life. You scare the wits out of her, because she knows how I feel about you. If she had her way, I'd be a nun, and we aren't even Catholic. I understand how she feels, but the decisions she's made should apply to her life, not mine. That's what I told her that day we had the big fight. It's over now for me. I have to live my own life, and you're a part of it. You're the biggest part.

"I'm glad I told you this, Garnet. I'm tired of carrying secrets on my back. I want to lay my burden down."

chapter 32

Raphaella's story explained a lot: her mother's opposition to the two of us being together and her claim that it wasn't personal; Raphaella's reluctance to share a big part of her life. And especially the men at Hannah's — the way they looked at her, as if she was Hannah come back to life.

As for her gift, as she called it, well, I had been aware of that for a long time. Her remarkable ability to sense and interpret things was something I was used to. As I slipped my hand over hers, I remembered that day in English class, the debate about love at first sight, and for the first time I wondered, How much had Raphaella known about me that day that I didn't know about myself?

"Hannah's murderers sensed your gift," I

said. "That's why they went after you. They thought you were like her, and they were right."

"I guess so."

"I wonder why Hannah didn't do something to fend them off, the way you did."

"From what you told me, they caught her by surprise and she had no chance to think or defend herself."

"No, she didn't," I said, recalling the kicked-in door, the terrified woman dragged outside and stoned. "She was a helper and a healer, skilled and knowledgeable, like you, and because of her knowledge they killed her."

I thought of my mother and the assault on her by the militia — I had told Raphaella about it — and once again I realized how much danger Mom had been in. Those men could have killed her. And they would have gone home at the end of the day telling each other and themselves that they had done the right thing.

2

"It's your deal, Gareth."

"Okey-dokey."

While Mom added up the score, my father began to show off, shuffling the deck like a Las

Vegas pit boss — until a few cards burst into the air and fluttered to the floor. He started again.

"What's the score, Mrs. Havelock?" Raphaella asked, smirking my way.

"Don't tell her," I said. "She'll only rub it in."

Raphaella had come over for dinner. Wearing a T-shirt with "Democracy: Use It Or Lose It" printed across the front in white letters, she had arrived on the front verandah carrying a package of sesame seed crackers, a small bouquet of flowers and a box of rosehip tea. It was a hot day, so we had eaten our salad and cold-cuts out on the patio. Dad and I had washed and dried the dishes — we lost the toss — while Mom and Raphaella set up the card table.

Raphaella and I were still learning the basics of bridge. To balance the skill level, she and Mom played against Dad and me. Mom played a conservative, calculated game. Dad took risks, playing with passion and energy. Raphaella and I stumbled along, trying not to make mistakes.

"Couldn't we switch to crazy eights?" I asked as Dad dealt our hands.

"Don't worry, podnah," he said, sorting his cards. "We've got 'em right where we want 'em."

"Then how come they're winning?"

"They're falling into our trap," he said.

"Before the bidding starts, your father has something for you," Mom announced.

Beaming, Dad slipped a small envelope across the table.

I gave Mom an enquiring glance. She raised her eyebrows but said nothing. Inside was a flimsy slip of paper.

"It's a receipt from, let me see, The Book Bindery," I read. "I don't get it, Dad."

"Read on."

In the space under "Description of item" someone had written, "Maitland Diary."

I handed the slip to Raphaella. Mom put down her cards and said, "The diary is being rebound. It should be ready in a few weeks."

"Then it's yours," Dad concluded. "The bookbinder will preserve what's left of the original cover and replace the missing part. It will be a refurbished artifact for Olde Gold's refurbisher."

"Dad, I . . . I don't know what to say."

"I saw you reading it that night in the shop," he said. "You got so involved you let your pizza get cold." He turned to Raphaella. "Can you imagine how interesting that diary must have been to make this guy forget his dinner?"

Raphaella looked me in the eye and smiled. "I think so," she said.

"Dad, Mom, I can't tell you how much this means."

My father waved off my words. "Take it easy," he said. "It's just a book, right?" And picking up his cards he added, "Let's play this hand. Your bid, Raphaella."

Raphaella fanned her cards, hesitated and, with a gleam in her eye, asked, "Um, can I bid two no trumps?"

I groaned. "Pass."

"Six no trumps," Mom responded.

"Pass," from my father.

"Seven no trumps," Raphaella said.

I led one of my thirteen useless cards and Mom began to lay down her hand, neatly arranging the rows on the green felt.

Raphaella nervously fingered her cards. I could tell she was reviewing what she'd learned about playing a hand.

"Take your time," Mom assured her. "And be careful."

"And no shenanigans," Dad put in.

Raphaella looked at me, then turned to my father.

"Shenanigans?" she said.

3

A few days passed before we got around to driving out to the Third Concession. Neither Raphaella nor I was anxious to return there, but we had left our equipment behind when we ran from the men.

"Besides," I said. "Aren't you curious to see if anything is different?"

When we got to the African Methodist Church I began to regret my bravado. I let the van roll to a stop and parked by the monument. It was the kind of summer evening when the air is soft, the sky taking on a pink band along the horizon, and you wish that time would stop. The building and cemetery looked peaceful, and the smell of freshly mowed grass hung in the still air. But my nerves didn't feel the calm.

I got out of the van and closed the door quietly. Raphaella stole a glance at the church, then looked away. I kept my eye on her as we walked across the old cemetery and climbed the fence. If there were any unwelcome presences around, she'd know, I figured. She turned to me and smiled as if to say, Nothing yet.

We plodded slowly through the trees, scanning

the forest on both sides of the path, our feet making the only noise. By the stream, where Raphaella had confronted the men, the mark in the earth when she clawed up the handful of dirt was still there. We continued, slowing as we reached the clearing. I took her hand and we held our breath in unison as we stepped out of the trees.

I was the first to laugh.

On the pile of rocks that had once been Hannah's chimney sat a grey squirrel, busily nibbling on a pine cone that he held between his little hands, as unconcerned as if he owned the place. Sparrows squabbled in the trees and darted across the clearing, chasing one another. Bees hummed and butterflies fluttered in the warm air.

"Well, I guess it makes sense," Raphaella said, reading my mind. "Hannah's gone. The others must be gone, too."

Our tent was half-collapsed, and stones lay scattered about. We set to work, rolling the tent and stuffing it into its bag, then packed our gear, including the little radio, into the backpacks we had brought with us. When we were finished, Raphaella took a look around and shouldered her pack.

"It seems so, well, normal here now. But I won't miss the place, that's for sure."

I stood quietly and looked at the only reminder that the men who had chased Raphaella and me away had been here. The thrown stones, which had been plowed up by Jubal and Hannah after they had cleared the land of trees, lay where they had fallen. I picked one up — it was cool and rough against my skin — and thought about the irony: with the man she loved, Hannah had labored to pull from the ground the instruments of her own murder. It seemed wrong to leave them scattered chaotically around her yard.

"There's something I want to do before we go," I said.

"I'll help."

"No, I'd rather do this by myself."

Raphaella nodded, sloughed of her pack and sat down on it, watching me. She smiled.

One by one I gathered the stones and returned them to the wall, arranging them in as orderly a fashion as I could to make the wall the way it had been. It didn't take long. When I had finished, I took Raphaella by the hand and we walked back through the woods.

Author's note

The black settlement in Oro Township in the nineteenth century and the African Methodist Church are part of the historical record. However, this remains a work of fiction, and names, characters, incidents and places are either products of my imagination or are used fictitiously.

Acknowledgments

Thanks are gratefully offered to my three children, Brendan, Megan and Dylan, and to Rachel McMillan and Leanne Dwinnell for reading the manuscript and offering suggestions; to John Pearce for support and guidance; and to Ting-xing Ye for comments, suggestions, love and inspiration.

In doing background research for this novel, I found these books helpful: *Men of Colour,* by David French (Kaste Books, 1978) and *The Oro African Church* by Tim Crawford (Township of Oro–Medonte, 1999).

The persons in my dedication, Irene and William ("Ding") Bell, are my late parents. They were the model for the three couples at the center of this book.